THE FRIEND

THE FRIEND

SIGRID NUNEZ

RIVERHEAD BOOKS - New York - 2018

Riverhead Books
Published by the Penguin Group
Penguin Group (USA) LLC
375 Hudson Street
New York, New York 10014

Copyright © 2018 by Sigrid Nunez
Penguin supports copyright. Copyright fuels creativity, encourages
diverse voices, promotes free speech, and creates a vibrant culture. Thank you
for buying an authorized edition of this book and for complying with copyright
laws by not reproducing, scanning, or distributing any part of it in any form
without permission. You are supporting writers and allowing Penguin
to continue to publish books for every reader.

Epigraph from *The Little Virtues* by Natalia Ginzburg, translated
by Dick Davis, reprinted by permission of Arcade Publishing,
an imprint of Skyhorse Publishing, Inc.

Library of Congress Cataloging-in-Publication Data

Names: Nunez, Sigrid, author.
Title: The friend / Sigrid Nunez.
Description: New York : Riverhead Books, 2018.
Identifiers: LCCN 2017011191 (print) | LCCN 2017016355 (ebook) |
ISBN 9780735219465 (ebook) | ISBN 9780735219441
Subjects: LCSH: Human-animal relationships—Fiction. |
Female friendship—Fiction.
Classification: LCC PS3564.U485 (ebook) |
LCC PS3564.U485 F75 2018 (print) | DDC 813/.54—dc23
LC record available at https://lccn.loc.gov/2017011191
p.   cm.

Printed in the United States of America
1   3   5   7   9   10   8   6   4   2

BOOK DESIGN BY LUCIA BERNARD

You have to realize that you cannot hope
to console yourself for your grief by writing.

Natalia Ginzburg, "My Vocation"

———————

You will see a large chest, standing in the middle of the floor,
and upon it a dog seated, with a pair of eyes as large as teacups.
But you need not be at all afraid of him.

Hans Christian Andersen, "The Tinderbox"

———————

The question any novel is really trying to answer is,
Is life worth living?

Nicholson Baker, "The Art of Fiction No. 212," *The Paris Review*

THE FRIEND

PART ONE

During the 1980s, in California, a large number of Cambodian women went to their doctors with the same complaint: they could not see. The women were all war refugees. Before fleeing their homeland, they had witnessed the atrocities for which the Khmer Rouge, which had been in power from 1975 to 1979, was well known. Many of the women had been raped or tortured or otherwise brutalized. Most had seen family members murdered in front of them. One woman, who never again saw her husband and three children after soldiers came and took them away, said that she had lost her sight after having cried every day for four years. She was not the only one who appeared to have cried herself blind. Others suffered from blurred or partial vision, their eyes troubled by shadows and pains.

The doctors who examined the women—about a hundred and fifty in all—found that their eyes were normal. Further tests showed that their brains were normal as well. If the women were telling the truth—and there were some who doubted this, who thought the women might be malingering because they wanted attention or were hoping to collect disability—the only explanation was psychosomatic blindness.

In other words, the women's minds, forced to take in so much horror and unable to take more, had managed to turn out the lights.

This was the last thing you and I talked about while you were still alive. After, only your email with a list of books you thought might be helpful to me in my research. And, because it was the season, best wishes for the new year.

There were two errors in your obituary. The date you moved from London to New York: off by one year. Misspelling of the maiden name of Wife One. Small errors, which were later corrected, but which we all knew would have annoyed the hell out of you.

But at your memorial I overheard something that would have amused you:

I wish I could pray.

What's stopping you?

He is.

Would have, would have. The dead dwell in the conditional, tense of the unreal. But there is also the extraordinary sense that you have become omniscient, that nothing we do or think or feel can be kept from you. The extraordinary sense that you are reading these words, that you know what they'll say even before I write them.

It's true that if you cry hard enough for long enough you can end up with blurred vision.

I was lying down, it was the middle of the day, but I was in bed. All the crying had given me a headache, I'd had a throbbing headache for days. I got up and went to look out the window. It was winter yet, it was cold by the window, there was a draft. But it felt good—as it felt good to press my forehead against the icy glass. I kept blinking, but my eyes wouldn't clear. I thought of the women who'd cried themselves blind. I blinked and blinked, fear rising. Then I saw you. You were wearing your brown vintage bomber jacket, the one that was too tight—and looked only better on you for that—and your hair was dark and thick and long. Which is how I knew that we had to be back in time. Way back. Almost thirty years.

Where were you going? Nowhere in particular. No errand, no appointment. Just strolling along, hands in pockets, savoring the street. It was your thing. *If I can't walk, I can't write.* You would work in the morning, and at a certain point, which always came, when it seemed you were incapable of writing a simple sentence, you would go out and walk for miles. Cursed were the days when bad weather prevented this (which rarely happened, though, because you didn't mind cold or rain, only a real storm could thwart you). When you came back you would sit down again to work, trying to hold on to the rhythm that had been established while walking. And the better you succeeded at that, the better the writing.

Because it's all about the rhythm, you said. Good sentences start with a beat.

You posted an essay, "How to Be a Flâneur," on the custom of urban strolling and loitering and its place in literary culture. You caught some flak for questioning whether there could really be such a thing as a flâneuse. You didn't think it was possible for a woman to wander the streets in the same spirit and manner as a man. A female pedestrian was subject to constant disruptions: stares, comments, catcalls, gropes. A woman was raised to be always on guard: Was this guy walking too close? Was that guy following her? How, then, could she ever relax enough to experience the loss of sense of self, the joy of pure being that was the ideal of true flânerie?

You concluded that, for women, the equivalent was probably shopping—specifically, the kind of browsing people do when they're not looking to buy something.

I didn't think you were wrong about any of this. I've known plenty of women who brace themselves whenever they leave the house, even a few who try to avoid leaving the house. Of course, a woman has only to wait until she's a certain age, when she becomes invisible, and—problem solved.

And note how you used the word *women* when what you really meant was young women.

Lately I've done a lot of walking but no writing. I missed my deadline. Was given a compassionate extension. Missed that deadline, too. Now the editor thinks I'm malingering.

I was not the only one who made the mistake of thinking that, because it was something you talked about a lot, it was something you wouldn't do. And after all, you were not the unhappiest person we knew. You were not the most depressed (think of G, of D, or T-R). You were not even—strange as it now sounds to say—the most suicidal.

Because of the timing, so near the start of the year, it was possible to think that it had been a resolution.

One of those times when you talked about it, you said that what would stop you was your students. Naturally, you were concerned about the effect such an example might have on them. Nevertheless, we thought nothing of it when you quit teaching last year, even though we knew that you liked teaching and that you needed the money.

Another time you said that, for a person who had reached a certain age, it could be a rational decision, a perfectly sound choice, a solution even. Unlike when a young person commits suicide, which could never be anything but a mistake.

Once, you cracked us up with the line *I think I'd prefer a novella of a life.*

Stevie Smith calling Death the only god who must come when he's called tickled you pink, as did the various ways people have said that were it not for suicide they could not go on.

Walking with Samuel Beckett one fine spring morning, a friend of his asked, Doesn't a day like this make you glad to be alive? I wouldn't go as far as that, Beckett said.

And weren't you the one who told us that Ted Bundy once manned a phone for a suicide prevention center?
Ted Bundy.
Hi. My name is Ted and I'm here to listen. Talk to me.

That there was to be a memorial took us by surprise. We who had heard you say that you would never want any such thing, the very idea was repugnant to you. Did Wife Three simply choose to ignore this? Was it because you'd failed to put it in writing? Like most suicides, you did not leave a note. I have never understood why it is called a *note*. There must be some who don't keep it short.

In German they call it an *Abschiedsbrief*: a farewell letter. (Better.)

Your wish to be cremated had been respected, at least, and there was no funeral, no sitting shivah. The obituary stressed your atheism. *Between religion and knowledge, he said, a person must choose knowledge.*

What a preposterous thing for anyone who knows anything about Jewish history to say, one comment read.

By the time the memorial took place the shock had worn off. People distracted themselves with speculation about what it would be like to have all the wives in one room. Not to mention the girlfriends (all of whom, the joke went, wouldn't fit in one room).

Except for the slideshow loop, with its hammering reminder of lost beauty, lost youth, it was not very different from other literary gatherings. People mingling at the reception were heard talking about money, literary prizes as reparations, and the latest *die, author, die* review. Decorum in this instance meant no tears. People used the opportunity to network and catch up. Gossip and head-shaking over Wife Two's oversharing in memoriam piece (and now the rumor that she's turning it into a book).

Wife Three, it must be said, looked radiant, though it was a cold radiance like that of a blade. Treat me like an object of pity, her bearing announced, hint that I was somehow to blame, and I will cut you.

I was touched when she asked me how my writing was going. Can't wait to read it, she said untruthfully.

I'm not sure I'm going to finish it, I said.

Oh, but you know he would have wanted you to finish. (*Would have.*)

That disconcerting habit she has of slowly shaking her head while speaking, as if simultaneously denying every word she says.

Someone semi-famous approached. Before turning away she said, Is it okay if I call you?

I left early. On my way out I heard someone say, I hope there are more people than this at *my* memorial.

And: Now he's officially a dead white male.

Is it true that the literary world is mined with hatred, a battlefield rimmed with snipers where jealousies and rivalries are always being played out? asked the NPR interviewer of the distinguished author. Who allowed that it was. There's a lot of envy and enmity, the author said. And he tried to explain: It's like a sinking raft that too many people are trying to get onto. So any push you can deliver makes the raft a little higher for you.

If reading really does increase empathy, as we are constantly being told that it does, it appears that writing takes some away.

At a conference once, you startled the packed audience by saying, Where do all you people get the idea that being a writer is a wonderful thing? Not a profession but a vocation of un-happiness, Simenon said writing was. Georges Simenon, who wrote hundreds of novels under his own name, hundreds more under two dozen pen names, and who, at the time of his retirement, was the bestselling author in the world. Now, that's a lot of unhappiness.

Who boasted of having fucked no fewer than ten thousand women, many if not most of them prostitutes, and who called himself a feminist. Who had for a literary mentor none less than Colette and for a mistress none less than Josephine Baker, though he was said to have ended that affair because it interfered too much with work, slowing that year's novel production down to a lousy twelve. Who, asked what had made him a novelist, replied, My hatred for my mother. (That's a lot of hatred.)

Simenon the flâneur: All my books have come to me while walking.

He had a daughter, who was psychotically in love with him. When she was a little girl she asked for a wedding ring, which he gave her. She had the ring enlarged to fit her finger as she grew. When she was twenty-five, she shot herself.

Q. Where does a young Parisienne get a gun?

A. From a gunsmith she read about in one of Papa's novels.

One day, in 1974, in the same university classroom where I sometimes teach, a poet announced to the workshop she was teaching that semester: I may not be here next week. Later, at home, she put on her mother's old fur coat and, with a glass of vodka in hand, shut herself in her garage.

The mother's old fur coat is the kind of detail writing teachers like to point out to students, one of those telling details—like how Simenon's daughter got her gun—that are found in abundance in life but are mostly absent from student fiction.

The poet got into her car, a vintage 1967 tomato-red Cougar, and turned on the ignition.

In the first writing course I ever taught, after I'd emphasized the importance of detail, a student raised his hand and said, I totally disagree. If you want a lot of details, you should watch television.

A comment I would come to see was not really as dumb as it seemed.

The same student also accused me (his words were *writers like you*) of trying to scare other people by making writing seem much harder than it was.

Why would we want to do that? I asked.

Oh come on, he said. Isn't it obvious? The pie is only so large.

My own first writing teacher used to tell her students that if there was anything else they could do with their lives instead of becoming writers, any other profession, they should do it.

Last night, in the Union Square station, a man was playing "La Vie en Rose" on a flute, *molto giocoso*. Lately I've become vulnerable to earworms, and sure enough the song, in the flutist's peppy rendition, has been pestering me all day. They say the way to get rid of an earworm is to listen a couple of times to the whole song through. I listened to the most famous version, by Edith Piaf, of course, who wrote the lyrics and first performed the song in 1945. Now it's the Little Sparrow's strange, bleating, soul-of-France voice that won't stop.

Also in the Union Square station, a man with a sign: Homeless Toothless Diabethee. That's a good one, a commuter said as he tossed change into the man's paper cup.

Sometimes when I'm on the computer a window pops up: Are you writing a book?

What does Wife Three want to talk to me about? I am not as curious as you might expect. If there had been a letter or some message from you, surely I'd be in possession of it by now. She may be planning some other kind of memorial, a collection of written remembrances, say, and if that's the case she will again be doing something you said you did not want.

I dread the meeting, not because I dislike her (I don't), but because I don't want to be part of any of these rites.

And I don't want to talk about you. Our relationship was a somewhat unusual one, not always easy for others to grasp. I never asked, and so never knew, what you told any of your wives about us. I was always grateful that, though Wife Three was never my friend like Wife One, at least she was not my enemy like Wife Two.

It was not her fault that your marriage entailed adjustments to your friendships, that is what marriages do. You and I were closest when you were between wives, periods that never lasted long, because you were, to an almost pathological degree, incapable of being alone. You once told me that, with few exceptions, such as when you were traveling on business, on book tour for example (and not always even then), you hadn't slept a night alone in forty years. Between wives, there was always some girlfriend. Between girlfriends there were one-night stands. (There were also what you liked to call drive-bys, but those did not involve sleep.)

A pause here to confess, not without shame: I never heard the news that you'd fallen in love without experiencing a pang, nor could I suppress a surge of joy each time I heard that you were breaking up with someone.

I don't want to talk about you, or to hear others talk about you. It's a cliché, of course: we talk about the dead in order to remember them, in order to keep them, in the only way we can, alive. But I have found that the more people say about you, for example those who spoke at the memorial—people who loved you, people who knew you well, people who are very good with words—the further you seem to slip away, the more like a hologram you become.

. . .

I am relieved that at least I am not invited to your house. (It is still *your house.*) Not that I have any particularly strong associations with the place, having been there only two or three times in the several years that it was your home. I do remember well my first visit, not long after you'd moved in, when I got a tour of the brownstone, admiring its built-in bookcases and handsome rugs laid over aged walnut floors, and being reminded how essentially bourgeois contemporary writers are. Once, over a superb dinner at another writer's house, someone brought up Flaubert's famous rule about living like a bourgeois and thinking like a demigod, though I've never seen how that wild man's own life could be said much to resemble that of any ordinary bourgeois. Nowadays (the table agreed) the feckless bohemian had all but ceased to exist, replaced by the hipster known for his knowingness, his consumer savvy, his palate and other cultivated tastes. And fair or not, asserted our host, opening a third bottle of wine, many writers today admitted to feelings of embarrassment and even shame about what they do.

You who had moved there decades before the boom were disheartened to see Brooklyn become a brand and wondered at the fact that your own neighborhood had become as hard to write about as it was to write about the sixties counterculture: no matter how earnest one set out to be, the ink of parody seeped through.

As famous as Flaubert's words are Virginia Woolf's: *One cannot think well, love well, sleep well, if one has not dined well.* Point taken. But the starving artist wasn't always a myth, and how many thinkers have lived like paupers, or gone to paupers' graves.

Woolf names Flaubert with Keats as men of genius who suffered fiercely because of the world's indifference to them. But what do you suppose Flaubert would have made of her—he who said all female artists are sluts? Both created characters who take their own lives, as would Woolf herself.

There was a time—quite a long time, it was—when you and I saw each other almost every day. But in the past few years we might have been living in different countries instead of only different boroughs, staying in touch regularly but mainly through email. In all of last year we met more often by chance, at a party or a reading or some other event, than by plan.

So why am I so afraid to set foot in your house?

It would undo me, I think, to glimpse some familiar piece of clothing, or a certain book or photograph, or to catch a hint of your smell. And I don't want to be undone like that, oh my God, not with your widow standing by.

Are you writing a book? Are you writing a book? Click here to learn how to get published.

Lately, since I started writing this, a new message has been popping up.

Alone? Scared? Depressed? Call 24 Hour Suicide Hotline.

The only animal that commits suicide is also the only animal that weeps. Though I've heard that stags brought to bay, exhausted from the hunt, with no escape from the hounds, sometimes shed tears. Crying elephants have also been reported, and of course people will tell you anything about their cats and dogs.

According to scientists, animal tears are tears of stress, not to be confused with those of an emotional human being.

In humans, the chemical makeup of emotional tears is different from that of tears that form in order to cleanse or lubricate the eye, say because of some irritant. It is known that the release of these chemicals can be beneficial to the weeper, which helps explain why people so often find that they feel better after they've had a good cry, and also, perhaps, the reason for the enduring popularity of the tearjerker.

Laurence Olivier was said to have been frustrated because, unlike many other actors, he could not make tears on demand. It would be interesting to know about the chemical composition of the tears produced by an actor and to which of the two types they belong.

In folklore and in other fictions, human tears, like human

semen and human blood, can have magic properties. At the end of the story of Rapunzel, when, after years of separation and misery, she and the prince find each other again and embrace, her tears flow into his eyes and miraculously restore the sight he had lost at the hands of the witch.

One of the many legends about Edith Piaf also concerns a miraculous restoration of sight. The keratitis that blinded her for several years as a child was said to have been cured after some prostitutes who worked in her grandmother's brothel, which happened also to be little Edith's home at the time, took her on a pilgrimage to honor St. Thérèse of Lisieux. This might be just another fairy tale, but it is a fact that Jean Cocteau once described Piaf as having, when she sang, "the eyes of a blind person struck by a miracle, the eyes of a clairvoyant."

But for two days, I went blind. . . . What had I seen? I shall never know. Words of a poet describing an episode from her childhood, a period marked by violence and squalor. Louise Bogan. Who also said: *I must have experienced violence from birth.*

I thought I knew the Grimm story by heart, but I had forgotten that the prince tries to commit suicide. He believes the witch when she tells him he'll never see Rapunzel again, and throws himself from her tower. My memory was that the witch blinded him with her nails—and she does threaten that the cat that got his pretty bird will scratch his eyes out, too. But it's because he jumps that the prince loses his sight. There are thorns where he lands, which pierce his eyes.

But even as a child I thought the witch had a right to be angry. A promise is a promise, and it wasn't like she'd tricked the parents into giving up their child. She took good care of Rapunzel, protecting her from the big bad world. It didn't seem altogether fair that the first handsome young man to happen by could take her away.

During the period in my childhood when my favorite reading was fairy tales, I had a neighbor who was blind. Though a grown man, he still lived with his parents. His eyes were always hidden behind large dark glasses. It confused me that a blind person would need to protect his eyes from the light. What could be seen of the rest of his face was rugged and handsome, like TV's Rifleman. He might have been a movie star, or a secret agent, but in the story I wrote about him he was a wounded prince, and mine were the tears that saved him.

———

"I hope this place is all right. It was so nice of you to come all this way."

The trip, as she knows, took less than thirty minutes, but she is a gracious woman, Wife Three. And "this place" is a charming

European-style café, just around the corner from your brown-stone. (It is still *your brownstone*.) A perfect setting, I thought when I entered and saw her at a table by the window—not using an electronic device like everyone else who was there alone (and even some who weren't), but instead contemplating the street—for such an elegant, pretty woman.

She's the kind of woman who knows fifty ways to tie a scarf was one of the first things you ever told us about her.

It's not so much that she doesn't look sixty as that she makes being attractive at sixty look easy. I remember how surprised we all were when you first started seeing her, a widow nearly your own age. We were thinking, of course, of Wife Two, and of others who were even younger, and how, given your proclivities, it was only a matter of time before there'd be someone younger than your daughter. We agreed that it must have been the battles of your second marriage, which you used to say had aged you ten years, that drove you into the arms of a middle-aged woman.

But even as I admire her—the freshly cut and colored hair, the makeup, the hands beautifully manicured as I know the hidden feet are beautifully pedicured—I am unable to suppress a certain thought, the very same thought I had when I saw her at the memorial event and found myself remembering a news story about a couple whose child had vanished while the family was on vacation. Days had passed, the child was still missing, there were no leads, and the shadow of a doubt had fallen on the parents themselves. They were photographed coming out of a police station, an ordinary-looking couple whose faces left no impression. What stayed with me was the fact that the woman was wearing lipstick and jewelry: a necklace—a locket, I think— and a pair of large hoop earrings. That, at such a moment, a person would trouble to put on makeup and jewelry astonished me. I would have expected her to look like a homeless person.

And now again, in the café, I think: She is the wife, she found the body. But here, as at the memorial, she has made every effort to look not just presentable, not just pulled together, but her best: face, dress, fingertips, roots—all meticulously attended to.

It's not criticism I feel, only awe.

She was different: one of the few people in your life who wasn't in one way or another connected to the literary or academic worlds. She had worked as a management consultant at the same Manhattan firm since graduating from business school. But hey, she reads more than I do, you used to tell people, in a way that made us cringe. From the beginning, polite but distant toward me, content to accept me as one of your oldest friends while herself remaining only my acquaintance. Better this by far than the mad jealousy of Wife Two, who demanded that you stop having anything to do with me or any other woman from your past. Our friendship in particular irked her; she called it an incestuous relationship.

Why "incestuous"? I asked.

You shrugged and said she meant that we were too close.

She never would believe we weren't fucking.

Once, when we were on the phone, I said something that made you laugh. In the background I heard her complain that she was trying to read. When you ignored her and kept laughing, she became incensed. She chucked the book at your head.

You said no. You would agree to see me less often, but refused to drop me completely.

For a while you put up with the rages, the flying objects, the screaming and weeping, the neighbors' complaints. And then you lied. For years we met on the sly, as if we really were secret lovers. Crazy making. Her hostility never waned. If our paths crossed in public, she would look daggers at me. Even at the memorial, she looked daggers at me. Her daughter—your daughter—wasn't there. I heard someone say she was in Brazil, on a research project, something to do with some endangered—bird, I think it was.

Much unhappiness between you and your estranged only child, even less forgiving of adultery than her mom was.

She doesn't understand, you said. She's ashamed of me.

(What made you think she didn't understand?)

But not a drop of resentment in Wife Two's in memoriam piece. You were the light and love of her life, she'd said, the best thing that ever happened to her. And now, they say, she's writing a book about her marriage to you. *A novelization.* Wherein perhaps I'll learn whether you ever told her that, in fact, we did fuck. Once. Years ago. Long before she met you.

Barely out of school yourself, you had just started teaching. I was not the only one of your students to become your friend, and it was in that same class that we both met Wife One. You were the department's youngest instructor, its wunderkind, and its Romeo. You thought any attempt to banish love from the class-room was futile. A great teacher was a seducer, you said, and there were times when he must also be a heartbreaker. That I did not really understand what you were talking about did not make it less exciting. What I did understand was that I craved knowledge, and that you had the power to transmit it to me.

Our friendship went on beyond the school year, and that summer—the same period when you began courting Wife One—we became inseparable. One day you startled me by say-ing we should fuck. Given your reputation, this should not have been a surprise. But enough time had passed that I was no lon-ger anxiously waiting for you to pounce. Now came this blunt proposal, and I didn't know what to think. I asked, stupidly, why. Which gave you a good laugh. Because, you said, touching my hair, we should *find that out about each other*. I don't think it ever occurred to either of us that I might refuse. Among all my desires at the time—and you could call it the most ardent time of my life—one of the strongest was to put my full trust in some-one; in some man.

Later, I was mortified when you pronounced it a mistake for us to try to be more than friends.

For a while, I faked illness. For a while longer, I pretended to be out of town. And then I really did become ill, and I blamed you, and I cursed you, and I did not believe you could be my friend.

But when finally we saw each other again, instead of the painful awkwardness I'd feared, something—a certain tension, a distraction I hadn't even been wholly aware of before—was gone.

This was, of course, precisely what you'd been hoping for. Now, even as you completed your conquest of Wife One, our friendship grew. It would outlast all my other friendships. It would bring me intense happiness. And I felt lucky: I had suffered, but unlike others I never got my heart broken. (*Didn't* you? a therapist once goaded me. Wife Two was not the only one who found something unhealthy about our relationship, nor was the therapist the only one to wonder if it hadn't been a factor in my remaining single all these years.)

Wife One. An undeniably true and passionate love. But not, on your side, a faithful one. Before it was over she had a breakdown. It is not an exaggeration to say she was never the same. But then neither were you. I remember how it tore you up when she came out of the hospital and immediately found someone else.

When she remarried you swore *you* never would. There followed a decade of affairs, most of them short-lived, but a few all but indistinguishable from marriage. Not one do I recall that did not end in betrayal.

I don't like men who leave behind them a trail of weeping women, said W. H. Auden. Who would have hated you.

Wife Three. I remember your telling us that she was a rock. (*My rock*, you said.) Oldest of nine children, who as a girl had had large responsibilities thrust upon her when her mother developed a disabling illness and her father struggled to hold down two jobs. About her first marriage I knew only that her husband had died in a mountain-climbing accident and that they had a child: a son.

This is the first time she and I have ever been alone together. Because I have only ever known her to be reserved, I am surprised at how talkative she is today, the espresso loosening her tongue like wine. She does that thing with her head, shaking it back and forth as she speaks, slowly back and forth—is she trying to hypnotize me? She seems nervous, though her voice is soft and calm.

You were not the first person in her life to commit suicide, she says.

"My grandfather shot himself. I was just a little girl when it happened and I have no memory of him. But his death was very much a part of my childhood. My parents never talked about it, but it was always there, a cloud hanging over the house, the spider in the corner, the goblin under the bed. He was my paternal grandfather, and it had been drilled into me that I should never, ever ask my father about him. After I grew up I did finally get my mother to open up a bit. She said his suicide was a total shock. There was no note, and nobody who knew him could come up with a single reason for him to do such a thing. He'd never shown signs of being depressed, let alone suicidal. Somehow the mystery made it worse for my father, who for a long time kept insisting there must have been foul play. My mother said he seemed to be more angry with his father for not explaining himself than for taking his life. Apparently, he expected reason from a suicide."

You, on the other hand, had always suffered from depression. And never worse, she says, than in those six months last year, when you could hardly get out of bed in the morning and didn't write a word. What was strange, though, was that you'd gotten over that crisis and, since the summer, at least, had been in good spirits. For one thing, she says, the long drought was over and, after many false starts, you were finally launched on something that excited you. You were at your desk every morning, and most days you reported that the writing had gone well. You were reading a lot, the way you always did when you were working on a novel. And you were physically active again.

One of the things that made you so depressed last year, she explains, was that you'd hurt your back moving some boxes and couldn't exercise for weeks. Even walking was painful. And you remember his mantra, she says: If I can't walk, I can't write. But that injury had finally healed, and you were back to your long walks and running in the park.

"He was back to socializing, too, catching up with all the people he'd been avoiding while he was depressed. And you know that he got a dog?"

You had, in fact, emailed me about the dog that you found early one morning when you were out running. Standing on an overhang, silhouetted against the sky: the biggest dog you'd ever seen. A harlequin Great Dane. No collar or tags, which made you think that, purebred though it was, it might have been abandoned. You did everything possible to find its owner and when that failed you decided to keep it. Your wife was appalled. She's not a dog person to begin with, you said, and Dino is a lot of dog. Thirty-four inches from shoulder to paw. A hundred and eighty pounds. Attached was a photo: the two of you, cheek to jowl, the massive head at first glance looking like a pony's.

Later you decided against the name Dino. He was too dignified for a name like that, you said. What did I think of Chance? Chauncy? Diego? Watson? Rolfe? Arlo? Alfie? Any of those names sounded fine to me. In the end you called him Apollo.

Wife Three asks if I knew a certain friend of yours who'd committed suicide just months before you did.

We never met, I say. Though you had told me about him.

"Well, that poor man was in terrible health. He had emphysema, cancer, angina, and diabetes—his quality of life was frankly rotten."

You, on the other hand, had been in excellent health. The

heart and muscle tone of a much younger man, according to your doctor.

A pause here, a near inaudible sigh as she turns her head to the window, eyes raking the street as if the answer she is looking for is surely going to appear; is just running a bit late.

"My point is, though he may have had his ups and downs and didn't enjoy growing older any more than the rest of us do, he really did seem to be thriving."

When I don't say anything—what should I say?—she goes on: "I think it was a mistake for him to stop teaching. Not just because it was something he loved but because it gave his life a structure that I know was good for him. Though I also know he wasn't as happy teaching as he used to be. In fact, he was always complaining. Teaching had become too demoralizing, he said, especially for a writer."

My phone pings. The message is nothing urgent, but I note the time with a ripple of anxiety. It's not that I have somewhere else I have to be, I've made no other plans for today. But it's been half an hour, our cups are drained, and I still don't know what I'm doing here. I keep waiting for her to bring up a particular subject, one that's delicate to begin with and that I'd find even harder to discuss because I have no idea what she thinks or even how much she knows. I can think of several good reasons for you to have kept her in the dark about, for example, the group of students who complained about being addressed as "dear."

I thought the students had handled things well. They sent their letter to you, and only to you.

You probably thought it was charming, they wrote. Demeaning was what it was. Inappropriate. You should stop.

Which you did, but not without sulking. A perfectly harmless habit, you'd been doing it for—how many years? Ever since you started teaching. And in all that time, not a single peep from anyone. And now everyone—every woman in the class (and, like most writing classes, this one was mostly women)—had signed the letter. Of course you felt ganged up on.

How petty, didn't I agree? Didn't I see how absurd and petty the whole business was? If only they'd get this worked up over their own word choices!

One of those rare times that we fought.

Me: Just because no one ever said anything didn't mean no one objected.

You: Well, if they didn't *say* anything, they didn't *object*, did they?

Stupidly (I admit this was careless), I brought up the famous poet who'd taught in the same program many years before, and who, when selecting students competing for a place in his class, required the women to be interviewed in person, so that he could choose them on the basis of their looks. *And got away with it.*

I thought your head would explode. Talk about invidious comparisons! How dare I suggest that you'd ever done anything like that.

Sorry.

But what you had done, over the years, was conduct a series of romances with students and former students.

You never saw anything wrong with this. (*If I thought it was wrong, I wouldn't do it.*) Besides, there was no rule against it. Which was as it should be, you said. The classroom was the most erotic place in the world. To deny this was puerile. Read George Steiner. Read *Lessons of the Masters*. I read George Steiner, who had been one of your own teachers, revered, beloved. I read *Lessons of the Masters*, and I quote: *Eroticism, covert or declared, fantasized or enacted, is inwoven in teaching . . . This elemental fact has been trivialized by a fixation on sexual harassment.*

Unsaid: I was a hypocrite. We both knew I used to be thrilled when you called me dear.

And allow you to point out: In no few cases, it was the student who seduced you.

But I remember there was one woman, early on, a foreign student, who'd rebuffed your advances and later accused you of punishing her by giving her an A minus instead of the A she deserved. As it turned out, this particular student made a habit of challenging grades, and the committee that investigated the complaint determined that the A minus was, if anything, suspiciously generous. Still: though romantic relations between teachers and students were not officially forbidden, your behavior showed a lack of propriety and of sound moral judgment and could not be tolerated.

A warning. Which you ignored. And got away with it.

It took years for you to change. Meaning, it took age.

You had just turned fifty. You had put on twenty pounds, which you would lose again, but not for some time. You arrived at the bar already tipsy, got totally smashed, spilled your guts. I wished you would stop. I hated it when you talked about women. It wasn't jealousy, not anymore, and I swear I'd long since made my peace with this side of you. What I hated was feeling embarrassed for you. You knew there was nothing I could do, but you had to show me the wound anyway. Even if it required indecent exposure.

She is nineteen and a half—still young enough for "and a half" to mean something. She doesn't love you, which you can bear (which, to be honest, you even prefer). What you can't bear is that she doesn't want you. Sometimes she fakes desire, though never wholeheartedly. Mostly she is too lazy to do even that. The truth is, she doesn't care about the sex. She isn't with you for the sex. The sex that she does care about, you know perfectly well, she gets somewhere else.

By now it has become a pattern: young women who are willing to fuck you but who share none of the desire that drives you to them. What drives them instead is narcissism, the thrill of bringing an older man in a position of authority to his knees.

Nineteen-and-a-half has your heart on a string. Tug, tug, this way—no, that way, professor.

You liked to say (quoting someone, I think) that young women are the most powerful people in the world. I don't know about that, but we all know what kind of power is being referred to.

Promiscuity had always been second nature to you (your father before you, it seems, had been the same). And given your looks, your gift for words, your BBC accent and confident style, you had no trouble attracting the women you were attracted to.

The intensity of your romantic life was not merely helpful but essential to your work, you said. Balzac lamenting after a night of passion that he'd just lost a book, Flaubert's insistence that orgasm was a drain on a man's creative juices—that to choose the work over the life meant as much sexual abstinence as a man could endure—these were interesting stories but, at bottom, silliness. If such fears were grounded, monks would be the most creative people on earth, you said. And after all, plenty of great writers were also great womanizers, or at least known to have potent sex drives. You write for two people said Hemingway, you said. First for yourself, then for the woman you love. You yourself never wrote better than during those periods when you were having lots of good sex, you said. With you, the beginning of an affair often coincided with a spell of productivity. It was one of your excuses for cheating. I was blocked and I had a deadline, you once told me. Not even half joking.

All the trouble your womanizing brought into your life was well worth it, you said. Of course you never seriously considered changing.

That change must come—and without your having any say

in the matter, either—was something you appeared not to have worried overmuch about.

One day, in a hotel bathroom, you receive a jolt. A full-length mirror positioned directly across from the shower door. Nothing *too* hideous for a middle-aged man. But, in the glare of the vanity lights, truth won't be denied.

That is not a body to turn any woman on.

A power has been taken away, it can never be given back again.

It felt, you said, like a kind of castration.

But that's what age is, isn't it? Slo-mo castration. (Am I quoting you here? Did I get this from one of your books?)

The pursuit of women was so much a part of your life, you could scarcely imagine doing without it. Who would you be, without it?

Someone else.

No one.

Not that you were ready to give up. For one thing, there were always whores. And the bedding of students was by no means at an end. After all, it wasn't as if you didn't already know that, to the young, even a man of thirty is over the hill.

But not till now had you had to be content with couplings in which the other submitted—submitted completely—completely without desire.

Another mirror: *Disgrace*, by J. M. Coetzee. One of your— our—favorite books, by one of our favorite writers.

David Lurie: same age, same job, same proclivities. Same crisis. At the beginning of the novel he describes what he sees as the older man's inescapable fate: to be the kind of john prostitutes shudder at *as one shudders at a cockroach in a washbasin in the middle of the night.*

In the bar, drunk, maudlin now, you tell me how you went to kiss your baby and she shrank from you. I got a neck cramp, she said.

Why don't you stop seeing her, I say—mechanically, knowing full well that you are incapable of sparing yourself far worse humiliation.

David Lurie is so appalled by his degraded state—no longer sexually attractive but still squirming with lust—that he finds himself musing about actual castration, the possibility that one might get a doctor to do it, or even, with the help of a textbook, do it oneself. For would that really be any more disgusting than the antics of a dirty old man?

Instead, he forces himself on one of his students, a cannonball dive into disgrace that will be his undoing.

This was a book that you read with your skin.

But you were luckier than Professor Lurie. You never knew disgrace. Embarrassment, often. Sometimes shame. But never true, irremediable disgrace.

Wife One had a theory. There are two kinds of womanizer, she said. There's the kind that loves women and the kind that hates them. You were the first kind, she said. She believed that women tended to be more forgiving, more understanding and even protective of your kind. Less likely when wronged to want revenge.

Of course, it helps if the man is an artist, she said, or has some other type of noble calling.

Or is some kind of outlaw was my thought. That type above all.

Q. What is it that makes a womanizer one type or the other?

A. His mother, of course.

But you made a prediction: If I go on teaching, sooner or later I will come to grief.

I feared so too. You were one of several Lurian friends I've known: reckless, priapic men risking careers, livelihoods, marriages—everything. (As to *why*, the stakes being what they are, the only explanation I've ever been able to come up with is: because that's how men are.)

How much of all this does Wife Three know? How much does she care?

I have no idea and no desire to find out.

As if I had spoken my thoughts, she says, "Let me tell you why I wanted to talk to you." At these words for some reason my heart starts to pound. "It's about the dog."

"The dog?"

"Yes. I wanted to ask if you would take him."

"Take him?"

"Give him a home."

It is just about the last thing I was expecting her to say. I feel equally relieved and annoyed. I can't do that, I tell her. There are no dogs allowed in my apartment building.

She gives me a doubtful look, then asks if I'd ever told you that.

I don't know, I say. I don't remember.

After a pause, she asks me if I know the story of how you got the dog. For some reason I shake my head. I let her tell the story I already know. When you decided you wanted to keep the dog, you and she had a big fight. A beautiful animal—and how could she not feel sorry for the poor thing, being abandoned like that? But she didn't like dogs, she never had, and this dog—he's not a bad dog, in fact he's a very good dog, but he takes up a lot of space. She told you she refused to share any responsibility for it—for example, when you had to go out of town.

"I begged him to find someone else to take him, which is when your name came up."

"It did?"

"Yes."

"But he never said anything to me."

"That's because he really wanted to keep the dog. And in the end he wore me down. But your name came up a few times. She lives alone, she doesn't have a partner or any kids or pets, she works mostly at home, and she loves animals—that's what he said."

"He said that?"

"I wouldn't make it up."

"No, I didn't mean—I'm just surprised. As I say, he never said anything to me, and I never even met the dog. It's true, I love animals, but I've never had a dog. Just cats, I'm a cat person. But in any case, I can't take him. It's in my lease."

"So you said." A tremor in her voice. "Well. I don't know what I'm expected to do." Her shoulders sag. She has been through a lot.

There must be plenty of people who'd want a beautiful pure-bred dog, I say.

"You think? Maybe if he was a puppy. But, you know, most people who want a dog already have one."

Isn't there someone in her family who could take him, I ask. A question that seems to irritate her.

"My son and his wife just had a baby. They can't have a gigantic strange dog in their house."

As for her stepdaughter: impossible. "She spends so much time in the field, she doesn't even have a permanent address."

"I'm sure there must be someone," I say. "Let me ask around." But in fact I'm not hopeful. She's right: Those who want a dog already have one. And everyone I can think of who doesn't have a dog has at least one cat.

"And you definitely can't keep him?" I ask, leaving unsaid my very strong opinion that this is clearly what should happen.

"I've considered it," she says, to my ears unconvincingly. "For one thing, it wouldn't be forever. The life span of a Great Dane is short, maybe six to eight years, and according to the vet Apollo is already about five. But the truth is, I never wanted him, and I especially don't want him now. If I ended up keeping him, I know I'd resent it. And I don't want to live with that. To always have that feeling, complicating my already complicated feelings about—" About you, she means but does not say. "It would be too much."

I nod to show that I understand.

"Also, I was planning to retire soon," she says. "And now that I'm on my own I think I'd like to travel more. I don't want to be tied down by a dog I never wanted in the first place."

I nod again. I really do understand.

Someone had suggested that she look into dog sanctuaries, but all the ones she contacted had long waiting lists. It pained her to think how you would feel about her giving your beloved dog away to a stranger, or taking him to the pound. "But I might have to. He can't spend the rest of his life in a kennel. Among other things, it's costing a fortune."

"You put him in a kennel?"

"I put him in a kennel," she says, bristling at my tone, "because I didn't know what else to do. You can't explain death to a dog. He didn't understand that Daddy was never coming home again. He waited by the door day and night. For a while he wouldn't even eat, I was afraid he'd starve to death. But the worst part was, every once in a while, he'd make this noise, this howling, or wailing, or whatever it was. Not loud, but strange, like a ghost or some other weird thing. It went on and on. I'd try to distract him with a treat, but he'd turn his head away. Once, he even growled at me. He did it sometimes at night. It would wake me up, and then I couldn't get back to sleep. I'd lie there listening to him until I thought I'd go mad. Every time I managed to pull myself together, I'd see him waiting there by the door, or he'd start keening like that, and I'd fall apart again. I had to get him out of the house. And now that he's been gone, it would be cruel to bring him back. I can't imagine him ever being happy in that house again."

I think of the story of Hachikō the Akita, who used to go to Tokyo's Shibuya Station to meet the train that brought his master home from work every day—until one day the man died suddenly and Hachikō waited in vain. But the next day, and every day after that, for nearly ten years, the dog appeared at the station to meet the train at the usual hour.

No one could explain death to Hachikō. They could only make a legend of him, erecting a statue in his honor, still singing his praises today, almost a hundred years later.

Incredibly, Hachikō does not hold the record. Fido, a dog from a town near Florence, Italy, waited every day for *fourteen* years for his dead master (air raid, Second World War) at the bus stop where he used to arrive home from work. And before Hachikō there was Greyfriars Bobby, a Skye terrier who spent every night of the last fourteen years of *his* life at the grave of *his* master, who'd died in Edinburgh, Scotland, in 1858.

It is interesting that people have always taken such behavior as examples of extreme loyalty rather than extreme stupidity or some other mental defect. I myself doubt reports from China of a certain dog said to have drowned itself out of bereavement. But stories like these are one of the main reasons I have always preferred cats.

"What about if you took him just for a while? Even that would be a big help. The landlord can't object if the dog's only visiting."

It's not just the landlord, I explain. My apartment is *tiny*. A dog that size wouldn't have room to turn around.

"Oh, but he's a guard dog. He needs exercise, of course, but not anywhere near as much as other breeds. Even off a leash he won't go far from your side. And you'll see, he's very obedient. He knows all the commands. He doesn't bark when he's not supposed to. He doesn't destroy things. He doesn't have accidents. He knows to stay off the bed."

"I'm sure that's all true, but—"

"He had a checkup just a few months ago. He's in good health except for some arthritis, which is very common in big dogs his age. Needless to say he's had all his shots. Oh, I know it's a lot to ask, but I really want to get the poor thing out of that damned kennel! If I bring him home, though, I swear he'll spend the rest of his life waiting by the door. And he deserves better than that, don't you think?"

Yes, I think, my heart breaking.

You can't explain death.

And love deserves better than that.

PART TWO

Mostly he ignores me. He might as well live here alone. He makes eye contact at times, but instantly looks away again. His large hazel eyes are strikingly human; they remind me of yours. I remember once, when I had to go out of town, I left my cat with a boyfriend. He was no cat lover, but later he told me how much he'd liked having her because, he said, I missed you, and having her was like having a part of you here.

Having your dog is like having a part of you here.

His expression doesn't change. It's the expression I imagine in the eyes of Greyfriars Bobby as he lay on his master's grave. I have yet to see him wag his tail. (His tail isn't docked, but his ears have been cropped—sadly unevenly, leaving one a little smaller than the other. He has also been neutered.)

He knows to stay off the bed.

If he climbs on the furniture, said Wife Three, all you have to do is say *Down*.

Since he moved in with me, he has spent most of his time on the bed.

The first day, after sniffing around the apartment—but in a listless way, without any real interest or curiosity—he climbed onto the bed and collapsed in a heap.

Down died in my throat.

I waited until it was time to go to sleep. Earlier he had eaten his bowl of kibble and allowed himself to be walked, but again without seeming to care or even notice what was happening outside. Not even the sight of another dog could rouse him. (He, on the other hand, never fails to draw attention. It will take getting used to, this feeling of being a spectacle, the constant photo-snapping, the frequent interruption: How much does he weigh? How much does he eat? Have you tried riding him?)

He walks with head lowered, like a beast of burden.

Back home, he went straight to the bedroom and threw himself on the bed.

The exhaustion of mourning was my thought. For I am convinced that he has figured it out. He is smarter than those other dogs. He knows that you are gone for good. He knows that he is never going back to the brownstone.

Sometimes he lies stretched full out, facing the wall.

After a week I feel more like his jailer than his caretaker.

The first night, at the sound of his name, he lifted his block of a head, swiveled it over his shoulder, and eyed me sideways. When I approached the bed, my intention to displace him no doubt clear, he did the unthinkable: he growled.

People have expressed astonishment at the fact that I wasn't afraid. Didn't I think he might do more than growl next time.

No. I never thought that.

But I did think of a twist on the old joke Where does a five-hundred-pound gorilla sleep?

It wasn't quite true what I'd told Wife Three, about never having had a dog. More than once I've shared a household with a person who owned a dog. In one case the dog was a mixed breed, half Great Dane, half German shepherd. So I was not entirely unfamiliar with dogs, with big dogs, or with this particular breed. I was aware, of course, of the passion the species has for our own, even if they don't all take it as far as Hachikō and his kind. Who doesn't know that the dog is the epitome of devotion? But it's this devotion to humans, so instinctual that it's given freely even to persons who are unworthy of it, that has made me prefer cats. Give me a pet that can get along without me.

It was entirely true what I'd told Wife Three about the size of my apartment: barely five hundred square feet. Two nearly equal-sized rooms, a kitchenette, a bathroom so narrow that Apollo enters and backs out of it like a stall. In the bedroom closet I keep an air mattress that I bought a few years ago when my sister came to visit.

When I wake it's the middle of the night. The blinds are open, the moon is high, and by the ample streaming light I can make out his big bright eyes and juicy black plum of a nose. I lie still, on my back, in the pungent fog of his breath. What seems like a long time goes by. Every few seconds a drop from his tongue splashes my face. Finally he places one of his massive paws, the size of a man's fist, in the center of my chest and lets it rest there: a heavy weight (think of a castle door knocker).

I don't speak, I don't move or reach out to pet him. He must be able to feel my heart. I have the appalling thought that he might decide to lay his whole weight on me, recalling a news item about a camel that killed its keeper by biting, kicking, and sitting on top of him, and how rescuers had to use a rope tied to a pickup to pull the beast off.

At last the paw lifts. Next, the nose, thrust in the crook of my neck. It tickles insanely, but I control myself. He snuffles all around my head and neck then along the entire outline of my body, sometimes nudging me hard, as though to get at something underneath me. At last, with a violent sneeze, he gets back on the bed, and we both go back to sleep.

It happens every night: for a few minutes I become an object of intense fascination. But during the day, he is in his own world and he mostly ignores me. What's it all about? I am reminded of a cat I once had that would never let me cuddle her or hold her on my lap; but at night, as soon as I was asleep, she would perch on my hip and sleep there.

Also true: the prohibition against dogs in my building. I remember when I signed the lease I didn't think anything of this.
I was moving in with two cats; the last thing on my mind was
getting a puppy. The landlord lives in Florida; I have never met
him. The super lives in the building next door, which is owned
by the same landlord. Hector is originally from Mexico. As it
turned out, he was in Mexico, for his brother's wedding, the day
I brought Apollo home. On the very day he returned, he ran into
us as we were going out for a walk. I rushed to explain: the
owner had died suddenly, there was no one else but me to take
his dog, who was staying only temporarily. An explanation that
seemed to me far more plausible than that I'd do something to
risk losing a rent-stabilized Manhattan apartment that, for more
than thirty years, even during times when I was living out of
town—because of a teaching job, say—I'd taken great care to
hold on to.

You cannot keep that animal here, Hector said. Not even
temporary.

A friend had told me about the law: If a tenant keeps a dog
in an apartment for a period of three months, during which time
the landlord does not take action to evict the tenant, then the
tenant may keep the dog and cannot be evicted for doing so.
Which sounded dubious to me. But it is, in fact, the law regard-
ing dogs in apartments in New York City.

Stipulation: The presence of the dog must be open and not
hidden.

Needless to say, there was no possibility of keeping this dog hidden. I walk him several times a day. He has become a neighborhood wonder. So far no one who lives in the building has complained, though no few startled at first sight of him, some even timidly backing away, and after one woman refused to squeeze into the small elevator with us, I decided we should always take the stairs. (Galumphing down the five flights he is a comical sight, the only time he ever looks ungraceful.)

If he were a barker, surely complaints would be many. But he is remarkably—disturbingly—quiet. At first I worried about the howling that Wife Three had told me about, but I have yet to hear it. I wonder if this is because he made a connection between howling and being banished to the kennel. Which may be a stretch, but that he doesn't howl anymore is one reason I believe he's given up hope of ever seeing you again.

You cannot keep that animal here. (Always *that animal*; sometimes I wonder if he even knows it's a dog.) I have to report.

I didn't think Wife Three was lying when she told me Apollo was trained to stay off the bed. She had made the assumption that he would adapt to a complete change in his surroundings without himself changing. I was not at all surprised when this turned out to be wrong.

I knew a cat whose owner had to give it up when her son became allergic to cat scurf. The cat was passed from household to household (mine was one of them) while a permanent home was sought. It survived two or three moves all right, but one more move and it was no longer the same creature. It was a mess—a mess no one was willing to live with and so the original owner had it put down.

They don't commit suicide. They don't weep. But they can and do fall to pieces. They can and do have their hearts broken. They can and do lose their minds.

One night I come home to find my desk chair on its side and most of what had been sitting on the desk scattered. He has chewed through a whole pile of papers. (I would honestly be able to tell my students, The dog ate your homework.) I'd gone out for drinks after class with another teacher, and we had lingered. I was gone about five hours, the longest I'd ever left him alone. The spongy guts of a couch pillow litter the floor. The fat paperback of the Knausgaard volume I'd left on the coffee table is in shreds.

All you have to do is connect with Great Dane groups online, people tell me, and you'll find someone to take him. But if you get evicted you won't find another apartment you can afford, not in this town. You might have trouble finding a place anywhere, with that roommate.

I keep having fantasies like episodes from *Lassie* or *Rin Tin*

Tin. Apollo foils burglars during attempted break-in. Apollo braves flames to rescue trapped tenants. Apollo saves super's little girl from would-be molester.

When you gonna get rid of that animal. He cannot stay here. I got to report.

Hector is not a bad person, but his patience is thin. And he doesn't have to say it: he could lose his job.

The friend who is most sympathetic about my situation assures me that it can take quite some time for a New York landlord to evict a tenant. It's not like you'll be put out in the street overnight, he says.

There's a certain kind of person who, having read this far, is anxiously wondering: Does something bad happen to the dog?

Googling reveals that Great Danes are known as the Apollo of dogs. I'm not sure if that's why you chose the name or if it was a coincidence, but at some point you probably learned this fact, probably the same way I did. I would also learn, in time, that Apollo is not an uncommon choice as a name for a dog or other pet.

Other facts: The breed's precise origins are not known. Its closest relation is thought to be the mastiff. And nothing Danish about it: *Great Dane*, it seems, was used by a misinformed eighteenth-century French naturalist named Buffon. In the English-speaking world the name stuck, while in Germany, the country with which the breed is most closely associated, it's the Deutsche Dogge, or German mastiff.

Otto von Bismarck adored the Dogge; the Red Baron von Richthofen used to take his up in his two-seat plane. First bred for hunting wild boar, later as a guard dog. And yet, though of a size that can reach over two hundred pounds and over seven feet tall standing on hind legs, known not for ferocity or aggression but rather for sweetness, calm, and emotional vulnerability. (Another, more homey epithet is "the gentle giant.")

The Apollo of all the dogs. After the one known as the most Greek of all the gods.

I like the name. But even if I hated it, I wouldn't change it. Even though I know that when I say it and he responds—*if* he responds—it's more likely to my voice and tone than to the word itself.

Sometimes I find myself wondering, absurdly, what his "real" name is. In fact, he might have had several names in his life. And what, after all, is in a dog's name? If we never named a pet it would mean nothing to them, but for us it would leave a gap. She doesn't have a name, someone says of an adopted stray, we just call her Kitty. A name, for all that.

I like that, well before T. S. Eliot expressed himself on the matter, Samuel Butler stated that the severest test of the imagination was naming a cat.

And your own LOL-inspiring thought: Wouldn't it be easier if we just named all the cats Password?

.   .   .

I know people who strongly object to pet-naming. They are of the same ilk as those who dislike the very idea of calling an animal a *pet*. *Owner* they don't much like, either; *master* makes them see red. What irks these people is the notion of dominion: the dominion over animals that humankind has claimed as a God-given right since Adam, and which, in their eyes, has always amounted to nothing less than enslavement.

When I said I preferred cats to dogs, I didn't mean that I liked cats better. I like the two species about equally. But aside from being unsettled by canine devotion, I, like many other people, balk at the idea of dominating an animal. And there's no getting around the fact that, even if you find calling dog owners slave masters ridiculous, dogs, like other domesticated animals, have been bred to be dominated by people, to be used by people, to do what people want.

But not cats.

Everyone knows the first thing Adam did with the animals that the Lord formed out of the freshly created earth—the first sign of his dominion over them—was to give each one a name. And until Adam assigned them their names, some say, the animals did not exist.

There is a story by Ursula K. Le Guin in which a woman, not named but unmistakably Adam's partner Eve, undertakes to undo Adam's deed: she persuades all the animals to part with the names they've been given. (The cats claim never to have accepted the names in the first place.) Once all have been unnamed, she can feel the difference: the downing of a wall, the closing of a distance that had existed between the animals and herself, a new sense of oneness and equality with them. Without names to separate them, no more telling hunter from hunted, eater from food. The inevitable next step is for Eve to give back to Adam the name he and his father gave her, to leave Adam and join all the others who, by accepting namelessness, have freed themselves from domination. For Eve alone, though, the act entails another renunciation, that of the language she shared with Adam. But then, one of her reasons for doing what she did in the first place, she says, was that talk was getting them nowhere.

He must have had obedience training early on, Wife Three said the vet said. Judging by his behavior, he'd been socialized both to people and other dogs. There were no signs of serious abuse. On the other hand, those ears: entrusted to some butcher who'd not only left them uneven but cropped each one too much. Those pointy little ears on his enormous head made him look less regal, and also meaner than he was, and were only one of several things that would have disqualified him from being a show dog.

Who could say how he'd come to be in the park, clean, well

fed, without collar or tags? Such a dog would not have run away from its owner unless something highly unusual had happened, said the vet. Yet not only had no one claimed him, no one had reported ever even having seen him before. Meaning he might have come from somewhere farther away. Stolen? Perhaps. That there seemed to be no record of his existence hardly surprised the vet. There were plenty of dogs whose owners never bothered to apply for a license, or, in the case of purebreds, register with the AKC.

Maybe the owner had lost his job and could no longer afford the food and vet bills. Hard to believe that someone who'd had him all his life would end up throwing him out to fend for himself. But: it happens more often than you might think, said the vet. Or say he had indeed been stolen, and the owner, on learning he'd been found, had had second thoughts. Life was easier without him, let someone else take care of him now! Again, the vet had seen it before. (So had I: Years ago my sister and her husband bought a second home, in the country. The sellers, who were moving to Florida, had an ancient mutt. A part of the family since he was a pup, they introduced him. When my sister and her husband went to move in, they were met by the dog, left behind, alone in the empty house.)

Maybe Apollo's owner had died, and it was whoever then came into possession of him who threw him out.

Most likely we'll never know where he came from. But here's

what you said. The moment when you looked up and saw him, majestic against the summer sky—that moment was so thrilling and so uncanny that you could almost believe he'd been magicked there. Conjured by a witch, like one of the giant dogs in the Andersen tale.

PART THREE

Rather than write about what you know, you told us, write about what you *see*. Assume that you know very little and that you'll never know much until you learn how to see. Keep a notebook to record things that you see, for example when you're out in the street.

I stopped keeping any kind of notebook or journal a long time ago. These days what I seem to see a lot when I'm out in the street is homeless people, or people who look so destitute I assume they're homeless. It's not unusual now to see such a person with a cell phone, though. And, unless I'm mistaken, more and more have pets.

On Broadway, at Astor Place, I see a dog all by itself surrounded by belongings: a full backpack, a few paperbacks, a thermos, bedding, *an alarm clock*, and some styrofoam food containers. It's the human absence that makes the scene so unbearably poignant.

I see a drunk who's pissed himself sprawled in a doorway. I Am the Architect of My Own Destiny, his T-shirt says. Nearby, a panhandler with a handmade sign: I used to be somebody.

In a bookstore: a man goes from table to table, laying a hand on this book then that one without examining any one of them further. I follow him for a while, curious to see which book this method tells him to buy. But he leaves the store empty-handed.

Here is something I did not see but would have seen if I'd rounded the street corner just minutes sooner: a person jumping from the window of an office building. By the time I got there the body had been covered up. All I was able to find out later was that it was a woman in her late fifties. Just before noon on a fine fall day, on a densely crowded block. How did she judge it, I wonder, so as not to hit anyone? Or was she just . . . were we all just . . . lucky.

Graffiti on Philosophy Hall: The examined life ain't worth it either.

A literary awards ceremony at a private club on the Upper East Side. I emerge from the subway at Fifth Avenue. The club is six blocks away. I see two people who've also just come up from the subway: a woman who looks to be in her sixties accompanied by a man about half that age. They could be going any of a million places in that neighborhood, but it occurs to me that they're headed where I'm headed. Which turns out to be correct. What was it about them? I can't say. It's an enigma to me that people in the literary world should be so identifiable. Like the time I passed three men in a booth in a restaurant in Chelsea and pegged them even before I heard one say, That's the great thing about writing for *The New Yorker.*

In the mail, an advance reading copy of a novel and a letter from the editor: I hope you'll find this debut novel as deceptively profound as I did.

Lecture notes.

All writers are monsters. Henry de Montherlant.

Writers are always selling somebody out. [Writing] is an aggressive, even a hostile act . . . the tactic of a secret bully. Joan Didion.

Every journalist . . . knows . . . what he does is morally indefensible. Janet Malcolm.

Any writer worth his salt knows that only a small proportion of literature does more than partly compensate people for the damage they have suffered in learning to read. Rebecca West.

There seems to be no remedy for the vice of literature; those afflicted persist in the habit despite the fact that there is no longer any pleasure to be derived from it. W. G. Sebald.

Whenever he saw his books in a store, he felt like he'd gotten away with something, said John Updike.

Who also expressed the opinion that a nice person wouldn't become a writer.

The problem of self-doubt.

The problem of shame.

The problem of self-loathing.

You once put it like this: When I get so fed up with something I'm writing that I decide to quit, and then, later, I find myself irresistibly drawn back to it, I always think: *Like a dog to its vomit*.

If someone asks me what I teach, one of my colleagues says, why is it that I can never say "writing" without feeling embarrassed.

Office hours. The student refers to a certain fact about his life and says, But you already knew that. No, I say, I didn't. He looks annoyed. What do you mean? Didn't you read my story? I explain that I never automatically assume a work of fiction is autobiographical. When I ask him why he thinks I should have known that he was writing about himself, he looks puzzled and says, Who else would I be writing about?

A friend of mine who is working on a memoir says, I hate the idea of writing as some kind of catharsis, because it seems like that can't possibly produce a good book.

You cannot hope to console yourself for your grief by writing, warns Natalia Ginzburg.

Turn then to Isak Dinesen, who believed that you could make any sorrow bearable by putting it into a story or telling a story about it.

I suppose that I did for myself what psychoanalysts do for their patients. I expressed some very long felt and deeply felt emotion. And in expressing it I explained it and then laid it to rest. Woolf is talking about writing about her mother, thoughts of whom had obsessed her between the ages of thirteen (her age when her mother died) and forty-four, when, *in a great, apparently involuntary rush*, she wrote *To the Lighthouse*. After which the obsession ceased: *I no longer hear her voice; I do not see her.*

Q. Does the effectiveness of catharsis depend on the *quality* of the writing? And if a person finds catharsis by writing a book, does it matter whether or not the book is any good?

My friend is also writing about her mother.

Writers love quoting Milosz: *When a writer is born into a family, the family is finished.*

After I put my mother in a novel she never forgave me.

Rather than, say, Toni Morrison, who called basing a character on a real person an infringement of copyright. A person owns his life, she says. It's not for another to use it for fiction.

In a book I am reading the author talks about word people versus fist people. As if words could not also be fists. Aren't often fists.

. . .

A major theme in the work of Christa Wolf is the fear that writing about someone is a way of killing that person. Transforming someone's life into a story is like turning that person into a pillar of salt. In an autobiographical novel, she describes a recurring childhood dream in which she kills mother and father by writing about them. The shame of being a writer haunted her all her life.

I wonder how many psychoanalysts actually do for their patients what Woolf did for herself. I bet not many.

They can debunk Freud's ideas all they want, you said. But no one can say the man wasn't a great writer.

Was Freud even a real person? I once heard a student ask.

It was a psychoanalyst, of course, who came up with the term *writer's block*. Edmund Bergler was, like Freud, an Austrian Jew, and he was a follower of Freudian theory. According to Wikipedia, he believed that masochism was the root cause of all other human neuroses, that the only thing worse than man's inhumanity to man was man's inhumanity to himself.

(But a woman writer has a double dose, said Edna O'Brien: the masochism of the woman *and* that of the artist.)

The invitation was to teach a writing workshop at a treatment center for victims of human trafficking. The person who asked was someone I knew, or rather, used to know: we had been friends in college. Back then she, too, wanted to be a writer. Instead she became a psychologist. For the past ten years she'd been working at the treatment center, which was connected to a large psychiatric hospital a short bus ride from Manhattan. The women she worked with had responded well to art therapy (I would later see some of their drawings and find them highly disturbing). She thought writing might be even more helpful, as it appeared to have been very helpful to other trauma victims, such as war veterans with PTSD.

I wanted to do it. As a community service, as a favor to an old friend, and as a writer.

I thought of the baroquely pierced and tattooed young woman I'd met some months earlier, in a workshop I'd taught at a summer writers' conference. It was a fiction workshop, though what she was writing was closer to memoir—call it autofiction, self-fiction, reality fiction, whatever—the first-person story of Larette, a sex-trafficked girl.

Her writing was good for three main reasons: a lack of sentimentality, a lack of self-pity, and a sense of humor. (If the last sounds unlikely, try to think of a good book that, no matter how dark the subject, does not include something comic. It's because a person has a sense of humor that we feel we can trust them, says Milan Kundera.) One of those life histories that had to be *toned down* to avoid straining belief. (Readers would be amazed how often writers do this.) She had spent two years in a residential recovery home, fighting drug addiction, shame, and the temptation to flee back to her pimp, whose name was tattooed in three different places on her body. Later, she enrolled in a community college, where she took her first writing course.

Like many people I've met, she believes that writing saved her life.

About writing as self-help you were always skeptical. You liked quoting Flannery O'Connor: Only those with a gift should be writing for public consumption.

But how rare to meet a person who thinks what they're writing is meant to stay private. And how common to meet one who thinks what they're writing entitles them not just to public consumption but to fame.

You thought people were on the wrong track. You thought that what they were searching for—self-expression, community, connection—would more likely be found elsewhere. Collective singing and dancing. Quilting bees. That's where people would have turned in the past, you said. Writing was too hard! Not for nothing did Henry James say anyone who wants to be a writer must inscribe on his banner the one word *loneliness*. Frustration and humiliation, Philip Roth said writing was. He compared it to baseball: *You fail two-thirds of the time.*

That was the reality, you said. But in our graphomaniac age, the reality had gotten lost. Now everyone writes just like everyone poops, and at the word *gift* many want to reach for a gun. The rise of self-publishing was a catastrophe, you said. It was the death of literature. Which meant the death of culture. And Garrison Keillor was right, you said: When everyone's a writer, no one is. (Though, in fact, this was exactly the kind of statement you used to warn us to be on guard against: *sounds* good, but if you press on it, it falls apart.)

None of this was as new as it might sound.

To write and have something published is less and less something special. Why not me, too? everyone asks.

Wrote French critic Sainte-Beuve.

In 1839.

Not that you discouraged me from teaching at the VOT center. I imagine it could be very depressing, you said, but it won't be uninteresting.

In fact, it was your idea that I should write about it.

The women at the center were encouraged to keep journals. Or, as my friend the psychologist put it, to journal. The journals were meant to be private, she said. Some of the women had been alarmed by the thought that someone might read what they'd written, and she'd had to assure them this wouldn't happen. They could write whatever they wished, with perfect freedom, knowing no one else would read it. Not even she would read it.

She suggested that those for whom English was a second language write in their native tongue.

Some women were careful to hide their journals when they weren't using them. Others carried their journals always with them. But a few insisted on destroying whatever they'd written immediately or soon after they'd written it. And that was fine, too, she told them.

The women were asked to write every day for at least fifteen minutes, quickly, not stopping to ponder too long or let themselves be distracted. They wrote in longhand, in notebooks provided by the center (my friend believes in studies that show longhand is better for concentration and that a lined page is more welcoming than a blank screen for receiving intimacies and secrets).

Of course, there were some who refused to journal.

The same women who get angry with me for expecting them to revisit bad experiences, she said. You have to understand what these women have been through. For most of them the abuse didn't begin with the trafficking. (*I must have experienced violence from birth.*) Some were deliberately put in harm's way— in some cases out-and-out sold—by members of their own family. And just because they're not being abused anymore doesn't mean they're not still hurting. At some point I always ask them what they think would be the best thing that could happen to them, and I can't tell you how many say, I think the best thing for me would be to die.

But there was a group of women who took happily to journaling, often writing for much longer than fifteen minutes a day. My friend wanted to give these women a chance to be in a workshop, a safe place where they could not only write but share their writing with one another and an instructor. Among those who'd signed up, she said, I could count on a certain level of English, though not every one was a native speaker. Even the native speakers, however, had expressed worries about their writing ability and were particularly concerned about spelling and grammar. She had told the women that, as in their journals, they should pay no attention to spelling and grammar.

So it's important that you ignore those errors, she told me. I know that won't be easy for you, but these women have enough problems with self-esteem, and we don't want to inhibit them.

I thought of a poem by Adrienne Rich that includes lines written by a student in the open admissions program in the City College of New York. *People suffer highly in poverty. . . . Some of the suffering are:*

My friend showed me examples of the artwork the women had done: headless bodies, houses in flames, men with the mouths of ferocious animals, naked children stabbed in the genitals or through the heart.

She had me listen to tapes of testimony some of the women had given, and the drawings came alive.

I keep calling them women, she said. But we see many who are still girls. And those are some of the most tragic cases. We have a fourteen-year-old who was rescued last month from a house where she'd been kept chained to a cot in the basement. When the sexual abuse is compounded by captivity—that's when the damage is most severe. At the moment this girl is unable to speak. There's nothing wrong with her vocal organs—not that doctors can find, anyway—but she insists on remaining mute. We see this kind of psychosomatic symptom from time to time: mutism, blindness, paralysis.

My friend wanted me to watch a Swedish film called *Lilya 4-Ever*. In fact I had already seen it, years ago, when it first came out. At the time, I didn't know that it was based on a true story. I didn't know much of anything about it; I had decided to see it one day on the spur of the moment because I had liked an earlier film by the same director and because it was playing close by. It is more than possible that if I had known what to expect I might never have gone to see *Lilya 4-Ever*. As it was, the experience was indelible: even more than a decade later, there was no need for me to see it again.

Lilya is a sixteen-year-old girl living with her mother in a bleak housing project somewhere in the former Soviet Union. She believes that she and her mother and the mother's boyfriend are all about to emigrate to the US, but when the time comes Lilya is left behind. Then a heartless aunt takes over the apartment where Lilya has been living, forcing her to move into what is no more than a filthy hole. Abandoned, moneyless, Lilya skids into prostitution.

From the people around her, Lilya has learned to expect only cruelty and betrayal. The exception is Volodya, a boy a few years younger than Lilya who is much abused by his drunken father.

Volodya loves Lilya, who befriends and shelters him after his father throws him out. Together the two waifs share a few happy moments. But, for the most part, Lilya's life is grim.

Hope arrives in the form of a handsome, soft-voiced young Swede named Andrei. He tells Lilya, who falls instantly in love with him, that, with his help, she can move to Sweden and start a new life. She jumps at the chance, in spite of what this will mean for Volodya, who in fact responds to the departure of his only friend in the world by killing himself.

Volodya continues to appear in the film in the form of an angel.

Lilya arrives in Sweden, alone (Andrei has promised to join her later), and is met at the airport by the man she's been told will take her under his wing. The man drives her to her new home, a tower apartment high above the street, and locks her in. Rapunzel, Rapunzel. He is the first to rape her. Lilya's new life has begun. Now day after day she is delivered into the hands of clients—a broad range of ages and types—none of whom allows either her obvious youth or the obvious fact that she is acting against her will to interfere with his lust. On the contrary, every-one behaves as if sex slavery is what Lilya has been put on this earth for.

The first time she tries to escape, Lilya is caught and beaten. The second time, she finds herself on an expressway bridge. Though help in the form of a policewoman is near, Lilya panics and jumps.

. . .

After she jumped, the girl on whose life and death *Lilya 4-Ever* was based was found to have on her body some letters she'd written. This was how her story came to be known.

When I saw the film, alone, at my small neighborhood art house, it was a weekday afternoon. Only a handful of people were in the audience. I remember, after it was over, having to wait so that I could compose myself before leaving the theater. It was a humiliating feeling. Several rows ahead of me sat another woman who'd come to the theater alone and who was now sobbing. When I finally left she was sitting there still, still sobbing. I felt humiliated for her, too.

According to my friend, *Lilya 4-Ever* has often been shown to humanitarian and human rights groups and in schools in areas where girls are known to be especially vulnerable to traffickers.

Not brutal enough was the response from a group of Moldovan prostitutes who were asked to watch the film.

Even more shocking, to me, was hearing the director say that he believed that God took care of Lilya (like Volodya, after her death she appears on-screen as an angel), that without this belief he could not have made the film. I think I would have killed myself, he said.

And what does this mean he thinks that those who are without such belief, those who not for one minute trust that God takes care of the Lilyas of the world, should do?

My friend said, For people who have themselves been victims of inequality and exploitation, like the people trapped in Lilya's slum, there might be some understanding for the way they mistreat one another. There might even be forgiveness, she said. But the depraved behavior of all those privileged members of the prosperous Nordic welfare state—this is harder to accept.

I once saw a photograph in a magazine: a long line of men snaking outside a shack being used by some teen prostitutes. I don't remember what part of the world it was. I do remember that there was nothing about the men to suggest anything out of the ordinary. Several of them are smoking cigarettes. This one is looking at his watch, that one is studying the sky, another is reading a newspaper. Overall, an air of patient boredom. They might have been waiting for a bus, or for their turn at the DMV.

My friend told me about another case. Again, doctors could find no injury or disease that would have prevented the patient from speaking like any normal person. But she would not speak. When it was suggested that she start journaling, she was enthusiastic. In a week she had filled a whole stack of notebooks. She wrote in an astonishingly cramped script, the tiniest letters imaginable, my friend said. Just watching her scribbling away was frightening.

Her hand ballooned, her fingers blistered and bled, but she wouldn't—couldn't—stop.

We never knew what she was writing because she didn't share it with us, my friend said. But I wouldn't be surprised if it was mostly repetition and nonsense. Fortunately, we were able to give her medication that helped her stop the maniacal writing and start speaking again.

According to Larette, she, too, had gone through a period of mutism. Whenever she tried to speak her throat would close painfully, as if invisible hands were choking her.

I would try very hard, in spite of the pain, but the most I could manage was a dry squeak, like an asthmatic mouse, which made people laugh. I was so ashamed that I stopped trying. When I wanted to communicate I'd use writing or some kind of sign language or silently mouth the words. Still, my throat hurt all the time.

In therapy, she remembers an incident that she hadn't thought about in many years. This involved her grandmother, about whom she tried to think as little as possible. When Larette was ten, her mother was stabbed to death by a boyfriend. There being no father in the picture, she was placed in the care of her grandmother. Larette referred to this woman, an increasingly desperate meth addict, as "my first slaveholder."

She was the first one to sell me to men. I remember we were sitting at the kitchen table, and she got up and went to the fridge. She opened the freezer and took out a Popsicle, which she unwrapped and broke in two. I remember it was cherry, my favorite flavor. She popped one stick in my mouth. Lemme show you, hon. She put the other one in her own mouth and went to work on it.

This was one of several memories Larette had doubts about including in her book. She was afraid it would sound too made-up. She kept deleting it, then putting it back in, then deleting it again.

I know another woman, a writer, who has at times made her living as a sex worker. She is against the latest thinking that says every prostitute must be seen as a VOT. She wants a firm line drawn between a slave and a free and willing worker like herself. Brothel raids, john stings, and public john shaming fire her outrage.

God save us from the white knights, she says. Why is it so hard to believe that we don't all need, or want, rescuing? But then, hasn't it always been impossible for society to accept that what a woman does with her body is strictly her own business.

A story this woman likes to tell concerns the French actress Arletty, who in 1945 was convicted of treason because, during the Occupation, she'd had an affair with a German officer. In her defense she said, My heart is French but my ass is international. (Actually, my friend prefers a different, more succinct version of Arletty's famous quip: My ass is not France.)

My friend the sex worker says she is amazed how naïve most women are. They have no idea that most men have had sex with

a prostitute, their own fathers and brothers, boyfriends and hus-
bands among them. I have heard Larette say the same thing—as
I have heard men say they are doubtful of men who claim never
to have paid for sex.

In a recent television documentary, a former prostitute who
worked out of a suburban motel explains that Monday mornings
were her busiest times: apparently nothing was so good for business as a weekend spent with the wife and kids.

I once asked my friend if she enjoyed being a sex worker. I
was pretty sure she'd say yes. But she looked at me as if she
hadn't heard me right. I do it for the money, she said. There's
nothing to *enjoy*. If I could make a living off writing, I wouldn't
do it at all. It's easier than teaching, she said.

I had to promise not to use anything the women in the workshop
wrote. But my friend the psychologist agreed to let me write
about her and the work she did. You, in your generous way,
pitched the idea to an editor you happened to have lunch with.
Soon I had a contract and a deadline.

Not long after we had graduated from college, my friend
published some stories. The magazines they appeared in were
small but prestigious, the kind of literary quarterlies that got
serious attention. One of the stories won a prize, and later that
year she was nominated for, and subsequently granted, a much
bigger prize given annually to promising young writers.

I want to know why she stopped writing.

It wasn't exactly a decision, she said. It was just something that happened. I'd started writing a novel and was having trouble concentrating, and someone I knew suggested that I try meditation. That's how I got into Buddhism. I spent a month at a retreat upstate learning how to meditate, and I've been doing it ever since. I know there've been plenty of writers who were into Buddhism—and who *doesn't* practice some kind of meditation or yoga these days? And I know there are people who say that meditation helped their careers. But from the time I started studying Buddhism I found it at odds with wanting to be a writer.

To clarify, though, I didn't ever stop writing. There was no need for me to do that. I journal, for one thing—in fact, I consider journaling a kind of meditation—and I write poetry. The things I see in my job every day are very disturbing, and I've found that poetry helps. Not that I ever write about my job. My poems tend to be about the beauty of the world—about nature, mostly. It isn't very good poetry, I know that, and I have no desire to share it. For me, writing poetry is like prayer, and prayer isn't something you have to share with other people.

It wasn't that I wanted to withdraw completely from the world. I wasn't about to become a Buddhist nun or anything like that. But as I say I started having doubts about becoming a writer. I didn't see how I could reconcile a literary career with the goal of freedom from attachment. Soon after I finished the

Buddhist retreat I did a residency at an artists' colony—I was hoping to get back on track with the novel. I remember looking at the other people there, some of whom were just starting out like me and some of whom were already established, and thinking about what it took—besides talent, of course—to succeed. You had to have ambition, serious ambition, and if you wanted to do really good work you had to be driven. You had to want to surpass what others had done. You had to believe that what you were doing was incredibly serious and important. And all this seemed to me in conflict with learning to sit still. To let go.

And even though writing isn't supposed to be a competition, I could see that most of the time writers believed that it was. While I was at the artists' colony, one of the writers there got an advance so huge it was reported in the *Times*. That night at dinner he said, There go my last two friends. He was joking, of course, but I have noticed that whenever a writer hits it big a lot of effort seems to go into trying to bring that person down.

Also, it seemed like money was in the front of everyone's mind. I didn't get that. Who on earth becomes a writer for the money? I remember my first writing class, the teacher said: If you're going to be a writer, the first thing you have to do is take a vow of poverty. And no one in the room batted an eye.

It seemed to me that everyone I knew who was a writer—which back then meant pretty much everyone I knew—was in a state of chronic frustration. People were constantly getting worked up over who got what and who got left out and how horribly unfair the whole business was. It was very confusing. Why did it have to be like that? Why were the men all so arrogant, and why were so many of them sexual predators? Why were the women all so angry and depressed? Really, it was hard not to feel sorry for everyone.

Whenever I'd go to a reading I couldn't help feeling embarrassed for the author. I'd ask myself did I wish that was me up there, and the honest answer was hell no. And it wasn't just me. You could feel it in the rest of the audience, that same discomfort. And I remember thinking, This is what Baudelaire was talking about when he said that art was prostitution.

Meanwhile I was still struggling with the novel. And then one day I said to myself, Say you don't write this book. Weren't there a zillion other people willing to bring novels into the world? Weren't there, in fact, already too many novels? Did I honestly think mine would be missed? And could I justify doing something with my life, my one wild and precious life, that I knew, undone, would not be missed?

Around this time I happened to hear some writer talking on the radio. I can't remember who it was, but for me it might as well have been God. I remember him saying that if in all the next year not a single work of fiction was published, instead of the staggering number of stories and novels we knew would be published, the effect on the world would be essentially the same.

Not true, of course, because I suppose there'd be a significant effect on the economy. But I knew what he was saying, and I felt as if he were saying it to me. Which is when I said to myself, You must change your life.

Not that I didn't have regrets. There were plenty of times when I had the very lousy feeling that I was just a quitter, too lazy or too cowardly to live up to my own dream. But if I needed proof that I'd made the right decision, I just had to look at my own reading. I used to be the most passionate bookworm, but over the years I've become less and less interested in reading, especially fiction. Maybe it has to do with the realities I see every day, but I started to feel bored with stories about made-up people living made-up lives full of made-up problems.

For a while I kept up. I'd buy a book that everyone was calling a masterpiece, or the Great American Novel or whatever, and half the time I wouldn't finish it. Or if I did finish it, I wouldn't remember it. Most of the time I'd forget a book almost as soon as I closed it. Then it got to the point where I pretty much stopped reading any fiction at all, and I realized I didn't miss it.

What if she hadn't stopped writing fiction herself, I asked. Did she think she would still have lost interest in reading it?

I don't know, she said. I just know I'm much happier doing what I'm doing now than I would ever be doing what you're doing.

Maybe it was a compliment that she felt she could say all this to me without worrying about hurting my feelings.

.   .   .

The student who graduates from a writing program and goes on to . . . renounce writing. You and I were familiar with the type. There seemed to be one in every class, and we always wondered: Why was it so often the one with the most promise? (Exactly the case of Wife One.)

Write about an object. Write about something that is, or was, important to you. The object can be anything. Describe the object, then write about why it's important to you.

One woman wrote about cigarettes. Her best friend, she called them. She'd started smoking when she was eight. I would never have survived my life without them, she said. I would rather smoke than do just about anything. Another woman wrote about a knife she had used to defend herself. She was not the only one to write about some kind of weapon. But about half the women wrote about a doll. All but one of the dolls came to a bad end. They were lost or broken or in one way or another destroyed. The one doll to escape such a fate was now hidden away in a secret place from where the writer hoped someday to retrieve her. That was all the woman would say. She shook her head when I reminded her that she was supposed to describe the object. If she did that she might draw down evil, she said. The doll would come to harm, she would never see it again.

.   .   .

Week after week, reading the women's stories on the bus ride home, they began to seem like one big story, like the same story told over and over. Someone is always being beaten, someone is always in pain. Someone is always being treated like a slave. A thing.

Some of the suffering are:

The same nouns: knife, belt, rope, bottle, fist, scar, bruise, blood. The same verbs: force, beat, whip, burn, choke, starve, scream.

Write a fairy tale. For some, a chance to fantasize revenge. Again, always a tale of violence and humiliation. Always the same vocabulary.

No writing is ever wasted, you used to say. Even if something doesn't work out and you end up throwing it away, as a writer you always learn something.

Here is what I learned: Simone Weil was right. *Imaginary evil is romantic and varied; real evil is gloomy, monotonous, barren, boring.*

This was the last thing you and I talked about while you were still alive. After, only your email with a list of books you thought might be helpful to me in my research. And, because it was the season, best wishes for the new year.

PART FOUR

It sounded so unlikely: a memoir about a love affair between a man and a dog.

The man: J. R. Ackerley (1896–1967), British author and literary editor of the BBC magazine *The Listener.*

The dog: Queenie, a German shepherd. Acquired at the age of eighteen months by Ackerley, at the time a middle-aged bachelor with a formidable history of sexual promiscuity who'd given up hope of ever finding a partner.

The book: *My Dog Tulip.* The change of name suggested by an editor who saw a problem with "Queenie" because Ackerley was known to be gay.

Naturally, it was from you that I first heard about Ackerley. A volume of his letters had just been published. Well worth reading, you said, like everything he wrote. But it was his memoirs that you called indispensable.

Find the right tone and you can write about anything: I was reminded often of this dictum while reading the book. "More than you want to know about what goes in or comes out of a dog's vagina, bladder and anus," warns one customer review. In fact, most of *My Dog Tulip* is about what Ackerley calls her heats. Though at times the reader can't help feeling it's inevitable and so might as well brace for it, no act of bestiality occurs. But to say the relationship was not intimate would be a lie. Ackerley himself admitted that he sometimes touched a sympathetic hand to the burning vulva the frustrated dog kept thrusting at him.

Consider rereading, how risky it is, especially when the book is one that you loved. Always the chance that it won't hold up, that you might, for whatever reason, not love it as much. When this happens, and to me it happens all the time (and more and more as I get older), the effect is so disheartening that I now open old favorites warily.

The prose style is just as fine, the wit as sharp, the story, if anything, even more compelling than I remembered. But something has changed. The second time, I don't find the author as likable. I find him even somewhat dislikable. His hostility toward women—had I missed that, or just forgotten it?

Women are dangerous, especially women of the working class. . . . They stop at nothing and they never let go.

True, Ackerley has little affection for humans in general. But the misogyny is clear. Women are bad *because* they are women.

An exception is made for Miss Canvey, the competent and compassionate vet who immediately diagnoses the cause of Tulip's behavioral problems as a matter of the heart: *She's in love with you, that's obvious.*

As is the fact that he's in love with her. But, obvious as this might be, I am bewildered by his treatment of her. Tulip's behavioral problems are severe. A holy terror of a dog, badly trained, nervous and excitable to the point of hysteria, unsociable. She barks relentlessly, and she bites. Her behavior is so bad that it damages Ackerley's relationships with people. Friends are dismayed that he won't do more to discipline her. He blames "the disturbances of her psyche" on her first home, where she was left too much alone and sometimes beaten. But he himself often succumbs to berating and striking her, even though he knows such punishment can only confuse her.

Frustration, rage, violence (his words). The pattern seems inescapable. When Tulip has a litter, intensifying the chaos already reigning in the Ackerley household, he sometimes cuffs the pups.

Hard not to conclude that, with better training, Tulip would have been a happier dog, and Ackerley's own life (to say nothing of his neighbors') would have been much improved. But he is another one who balks at domination. Fixed in his head is the

idea that Tulip must enjoy a full canine life. Meaning she must
be allowed to hunt and eat rabbits, she must experience sex and
motherhood. But, even after one litter, he can't bring himself to
have her spayed: *How can I tamper with such a beautiful beast?*
Despite twinges of conscience, he is able to care less about the
fates of the mongrel pups for which he knows he won't find
good homes. The beloved's needs are all. Her heats not only turn
both their lives upside down, they create havoc for his entire
London district, given the large number of dogs that, like Tulip
herself *even in heat*, go outdoors unleashed.

Page after page on the torments of her sexual frustration.
Ackerley shares her pain, it breaks his heart. Season after season
they suffer together. Still he won't have her spayed. His descrip-
tions of this part of Tulip's existence are so harrowing that I
wanted to scream: How can you *not* tamper with her?

Much as you admired the work, I recall, you were repulsed
by the life. A life in which a person's most significant relationship is with a dog—what could be sadder, you said. But, to me,
it seemed that Ackerley had experienced to the fullest the kind
of mutual unconditional love that everyone craves but most
people never know. (How many have found their Tulip? asks
Auden.) A fifteen-year marriage, the happiest years of his life,
Ackerley said. And when the agonies of her last illness forced
him to have her destroyed: *I would have immolated myself as a
suttee.* Instead he carried on. He wrote, he drank. Six slow dark
years. He drank and drank, and died.

.   .   .

Man and dog. Did it really all begin, as animal experts think, with nursing mothers taking orphaned wolf cubs to their breasts to suckle along with their babies? And doesn't this fit nicely with the myth of the twin founders of Rome? Romulus and Remus, abandoned at birth, warmed and suckled by a she-wolf.

A pause here to wonder why we call a womanizer a wolf. Given that the wolf is known for being a loyal, monogamous mate and devoted parent.

I like that the Aborigines say dogs make people human. Also (though I can't remember who said it): The thing that keeps me from becoming a complete misanthrope is seeing how much dogs love men.

Oversensitive to smells in general and squeamish about the human body, Ackerley was not put off by any scent of Tulip's, not even from her anal glands, and saw prettiness even in the way she took a shit.

He writes less about her excretory habits than about her sex life. But that's still quite a lot. And it's the details. . . .

"Liquids and Solids" that chapter is called.

Though I always walk Apollo on a leash, I worry, just as Ackerley did, that a dog doing its business in the street—especially a big dog—could get hit by a car. Unfortunately, Apollo often squats a dangerous distance from the curb. I cannot, like Ackerley, solve the problem by letting Apollo use the sidewalk, even if, unlike Ackerley, I am always diligent in cleaning up the mess. My solution, whenever Apollo positions himself far enough from the curb to be in harm's way, is to position myself between him and oncoming traffic. It's true that now I've only put myself in harm's way, but I figure, I hope not too innocently, that a driver will take greater care to avoid hitting a human being. Manhattan drivers are not a patient lot. Many an inconvenienced one has cursed me. But there are others, I know, who would've slowed down anyway, as so many pedestrians do, to stare.

In "How to Be a Flâneur," you said you did not consider a long walk with a dog genuine flânerie because it was not the same as aimless wandering, and being responsible for a dog prevented a person from falling into abstraction. These days I spend so much time walking Apollo I can't imagine going out just to walk by myself. What prevents me from falling into abstraction, though, or doing much thinking at all, is the way he draws attention. I don't welcome strangers' attention at any time, but although Apollo shows no sign of being bothered by the lack of privacy when he takes a shit I find these moments especially trying. Worst of all is being watched while I'm cleaning up after him, which seems to give a certain type of person a charge. People comment on the size of his turds as if I were not standing right there with pail and shovel (in themselves the cause of much glee, though I was actually quite pleased with myself for coming up with the idea of using a child's sand pail, lined with a plastic bag, and a small garden trowel).

I feel sorry for you, someone says (grinning). Or: I love dogs but I could never do what you're doing.

A few people have chided me for having such a dog at all: Big dogs don't belong in the city!

I think it's cruel, said one woman. Keeping a dog that size cooped up in an apartment.

Oh, but we're just down for the day, I sang back at her. We fly home to the mansion tomorrow.

(Yes, of course, there are also nice people, above all other dog owners, any number of people who either mind their own business or say nice, friendly, intelligent things. But we all know niceness is never as interesting to write, or read, about.)

Liquids: When I see the gallons pouring out I'm grateful that he doesn't lift his leg like most male dogs; instead of a hubcap he might drench a window.

Solids: enough said.

And there's something *between* liquids and solids, the curse of large breeds. I have to mop his face several times a day. I call it swabbing the decks.

Rather than take him to his old vet, which would've meant finding a way to transport him to Brooklyn, I find one within walking distance of home. He is good with Apollo, but I am wary of him, the sort of man who speaks to women as if they are idiots and to older women as if they are deaf idiots.

When I tell him that Apollo never plays with other dogs, not even at the dog park, he says, Well, he's not so young anymore, is he. I'm sure you don't run and jump around the way you used to, either.

He shrugs when he hears the whole story. People throw pets out all the time, he says. It's the dogs who'd die for the owners, not vice versa. (Obviously he has not read Ackerley.) Doesn't the divorce rate tell us just how much the loyalty of a human being is worth? he says in a tone I find disquieting.

Someone once told me that many vets tend to be irritable because their profession exposes them to a particularly wide swath of human silliness—much of it, no doubt, in the form of anthropomorphism. I remember one who rolled his eyes when I said that my cat purred all the time so he must be happy. Purring is just a noise they make, it does not mean they're *happy*, he snapped.

This one tells me bluntly that although Apollo is in pretty good shape for his age he won't be long-lived. And given his arthritis, he says, believe me he wouldn't want to be. Whatever you do, don't let him gain weight.

He shakes his head at the botched ear job and points out what else makes him a less-than-perfect specimen of the breed: chest and shoulders too broad in relation to hindquarters; neck not quite pure white, and not quite the right distribution of black patches elsewhere on the body; eyes a little too close; jaws a little too wide; legs on the thick side. Powerfully built but stocky over-all, lacking true elegance.

He has no trouble believing that the dog is in mourning for his previous owner and that his emotions have been exacerbated by too many changes in his environment. (How would *you* feel? he asks roughly, as if this were a thought I would never have ar-rived at by myself.) I tell him about the howling, and about the awful new symptom that seems to have replaced it: Now and then Apollo is seized by a kind of fit. He looks all around as if befuddled. Then, tail clamped between legs, he crouches as close to the floor as possible without actually lying down. It's as if he's trying to make himself as small as he can. Then the shakes begin. For periods that last from a few minutes to as long as half an hour, he cowers and shivers uncontrollably.

Anyone would say he thinks something terrible is about to happen to him, I tell the vet, keeping to myself that these attacks are so disturbing to watch that they sometimes bring me to tears.

There are drugs to treat canine anxiety and depression, but this vet is no fan of them. It can take weeks for a drug to become effective, he says, and often it turns out not to be effective at all.

Let's leave that as a last resort, he says. For now, don't ever leave him alone too long, and be sure you talk to him. Exercise him as much as possible. You might also try massage, if he'll let you. Just don't expect him to change into Mr. Happy Dog. He may never recover, no matter what you do. And you'll never know why. It's not just that you don't know his history. People think dogs are simple, and we like to believe we know what goes on in their heads. But in fact we're finding out that dogs are a lot more mysterious and complicated than we ever thought, and unless they develop our language we'll never know them at all. Which goes for any animal, of course.

He's a good dog, but I have to warn you, he says. You're a little lady, he must outweigh you by eighty pounds. (This was flattering.) The way to deal with these large powerful breeds is to keep them from knowing the truth, which is that you can't really make them do anything they don't want to do.

As if Apollo doesn't already know that. More than once when we've been out walking he's decided we've walked enough. He stops and sits or lies down on the ground, and nothing I do can get him up again. I'm less angry with him than with the people who stop to watch and sometimes laugh. Once, a man, thinking to help, stood some distance away, patting his leg and whistling. Like rolling thunder came the response, new to my ears, and so menacing that the man and several other people nearby quickly crossed the street.

Whoever trained him made him understand that humans are the alphas, the vet says, and you don't want him to start thinking otherwise. You don't want him getting it into his head that he's the alpha. When he leans against you, the way Danes do, stand your ground, don't let him knock you over. Get him to lie on his back, spend a little time rubbing his chest. And for

God's sake, get yourself back on the bed and him on the floor. You train a dog by keeping him *down*.

My expression when I hear this clearly exasperates him.

He's a good dog, he repeats, quite loudly this time. Don't turn him into a bad one. A bad dog can easily turn into a dangerous one.

By the time he finishes examining Apollo and lecturing me, I like Grumpy Vet better. Though not so much his parting remark: Remember, the last thing you want is for him to start thinking you're his bitch.

Now that I have Apollo I often think of Beau, the Dane-shepherd cross that belonged to the boyfriend I lived with when I was in my early twenties. Still a puppy when I first met him, he grew up to be almost but not quite as tall as a Dane and with many of a Dane's traits but with a shepherd's nerves and aggression. Big, unneutered, and very dominant, he hit the street like someone looking for a fight (and often, alas, finding one). Our apartment was in a dicey neighborhood, but so long as Beau was behind it we didn't always bother to lock the door. I would take him with me to a friend's place two miles away, stay until one or two in the morning, then walk back home along dark and empty streets. Beau knew about the potential danger, you could see it in his tension, his hypervigilance; he was like a fur soldier; he was *cocked*, like a soldier's gun. More than once he terrified the wits out of some guy loitering on a corner, or in a building doorway.

(I should say that few people I knew living in that part of town in those years had not been the victim of a mugging, or a burglary, or worse.) There was something undeniably thrilling about Beau's rumbling barks and growls, the stance he took between me and whatever he saw as a threat (which included any strange man who so much as looked at me), the knowledge that he would defend me—to the death if he had to. It was all part of why I loved him.

Also, back then, I *liked* the way we attracted attention.

But things are different now. The city has calmed down, the streets are safe, and I don't walk around late at night anymore anyway. At one or two in the morning I am asleep. I don't need protection. I don't need a badass dog to defend me. I don't want Apollo ever to feel that he has to bark or growl at anyone. I don't want him to worry. I don't want him to be anxious. I want him to feel that we are both perfectly safe, no matter where we go. I don't want him to be my bodyguard. I don't want him to be my gun. I want him to chill. I want him to be Mr. Happy Dog.

He missed you, the woman who lives in the apartment above mine says.

Coming home from school, I ran into her at the elevator.

Meaning: Apollo is howling again.

He has to forget you. He has to forget you and fall in love with me. That's what has to happen.

PART FIVE

"Did you read about the Tibetan mastiffs?"

I had indeed read the article in the *Times*, and I say so, but the woman's need to vent is too great: she tells the story anyway.

Only a few years ago, in China, the Tibetan mastiff was a status symbol, a luxury item priced at the equivalent of an average of $200,000 with some puppies said to sell for more than a million. As the mania peaked, more and more dogs were produced by grasping breeders. Then the mania died. Worth too little, eating too much, the huge and sometimes hard to control dogs were no longer wanted. What came next: Mass abandonment. Dogs packed into transport trucks, where they suffered horribly and many died. The slaughterhouse.

Truly, not a story I needed to hear twice.

The woman is someone we often meet when she's out walking her own two dogs, gentle mutts, mother and daughter. From the news story she goes into her screed—it too is something she's shared with me before—about the evils of dog breeding. Mutts are what nature intended, mutts are what should exist. But what've we got instead? Idiot collies, neurotic shepherds, murderous Rottweilers, deaf Dalmatians, and Labs so calm you could shoot a gun at them and they wouldn't suspect danger. Fur vegetables, cripples, morons, sociopaths, dogs with bones too thin or flesh too fat. *That's* what you get when you breed dogs for the traits *people* want them to have. It should be a crime. (I thought this woman was crazy when she told me about pointers that freeze in point posture and then can't get out, but this grotesquerie turns out to be fact.)

I shudder to think what it'll be like fifty or a hundred years from now, says the woman, looking very dark indeed. But by then, she adds, the whole earth will have been destroyed. And, perhaps consoled by this thought, she takes her mutts and moves on.

I am left thinking about the mastiffs. Besides their great bulk and a mane that makes them look part lion, they are known for being fiercely protective and loyal to their masters. So what does a dog bred for those traits feel when its master lets it be herded onto one of those transport trucks? Does a dog understand betrayal? I think probably not. I think the main thing on the mastiff's mind, all the way to the slaughterhouse, is Who will protect Master now?

A digression. About animal suffering, what do we really know? There is evidence that dogs and other animals have a higher tolerance for pain than humans do. But their true capacity for suffering—like the true measure of their intelligence—must remain a mystery.

Ackerley believed that being so emotionally involved with people and trying forever to please them made a dog's life chronically anxious and stressed. But did they get headaches? he wondered, not even that much about them being known.

Another question: Why do people often find animal suffering harder to accept than the suffering of other human beings?

Take Robert Graves, writing about the Somme: *The number of dead horses and mules shocked me; human corpses were all very well, but it seemed wrong for animals to be dragged into the war like this.*

Why, of all the terrible memories of his ordeal as a POW in Japan during World War Two, was Olympic athlete and US Army airman Louis Zamperini most haunted by the memory of a guard torturing a duck?

Of course, in each of these cases the suffering was caused by human behavior, in the case of the duck an act of pure sadism. But aren't animals always at our mercy, and doesn't the pity we feel for them have to do with our understanding that the animal itself has no way of knowing the reason for its pain (a fact that makes some people insist that animals must suffer even worse than humans do). I believe the intensity of the pity you feel for an

animal has to do with how it evokes pity for yourself. I believe
we must all retain, throughout our whole lives, a powerful memory of those early moments of life, a time when we were as much
animal as human, the overwhelming feelings of helplessness and
vulnerability and mute fear, and the yearning for the protection
that our instinct tells us is there, if we could just cry loudly
enough. Innocence is something we humans pass through and
leave behind, unable to return. But animals live and die in that
state, and seeing innocence violated in the form of cruelty to a
mere duck can seem like the most barbaric act in the world. I
know people who are outraged by this sentiment, calling it cyn-
ical, misanthropic, and perverse. But I believe the day when we
are no longer capable of feeling it will be a terrible day for every
living being, that our downward slide into violence and barbar-
ity will be only that much quicker.

When people ask me why I stopped having cats I don't always
give the true answer, which has to do with how the ones I did
have died. Suffered and died.

All pet owners go through this. Your pet is sick, obviously
sick, but what is it, what's wrong? It can't say.

The intolerable thought that your dog, who believes you are
God, believes you have the power to stop the pain, but for some
reason (did he somehow displease you?) refuse to do so.

The poet Rilke once reported seeing a dying dog give its mistress a look full of reproach. Later, he gave this experience to the narrator of a novel: *He was convinced I could have prevented it. It was now clear that he had always overrated me. And there was no time left to explain it to him. He continued to gaze at me, surprised and solitary, until it was over.*

The suspicion that your cat, proud independent stoic that she is, is hiding just how bad things really are.

The trip to the vet, the diagnosis, well, that at least, at last. Surgery, drugs. (Stop spitting out those goddamn pills!) Hope. Then doubts. How do I know if she's in pain, and how much pain? Am I being selfish? Would she rather be dead?

Over the years, I've been there, several times, too many times, holding a cat that, the vet assures me, will go gently. My mother, who has been there too, said, The little honey lay in my arms the whole time, right up to the end, purring. (I know: that's just a noise they make.)

Shortly after one of my last two cats died (in my arms, but not purring)—a cat I'd lived with for twenty years, longer than I've lived with any person—the surviving cat got sick. She paced the apartment, unable to rest, not for a single minute. Imagine: a sleepless cat. She wanted to eat, she tried to eat, but she couldn't. Her voice had changed, always now the same troubled and insistent mewing: Help me, why won't you help me.

The ultrasound revealed a mass. We could operate, said the vet, a soft young woman in assuringly rose-colored scrubs. But consider her age. I did, as well as how much she was already suffering, and the fact that, at nineteen, she might not survive an operation. The other option, said the vet, is to put her to sleep.

How Ackerley loathed that "dishonest" euphemism. But his word—*destroyed*—has always sounded odd to me when used for a sentient being. And neither he nor anyone else ever uses the honest *kill*. I had my dog Tulip *killed*. I took my cat to the vet to be *killed*. It would be better to have the poor thing *killed*. There's no hope, she needs to be *killed*. If we can't find them homes, they'll all be *killed*.

Do you want to be with her?

Of course.

Two injections, the vet explained. The first one is to calm her. . . .

The first injection was problematic. Something about dehydration and how that affected the veins. And now the cat, who until that moment had kept herself very still, grew alert. She stretched out a paw and touched my wrist. She lifted her head, wobbly on its frail stalk of a neck, and gave me a disbelieving stare.

I'm not saying this is what she said, I'm saying this is what I heard:

Wait, you're making a mistake. I didn't say I wanted you to *kill* me, I said I wanted you to make me feel better.

The vet was clearly flustered now. Before I could say a word, she scooped up the cat and headed for the door: I'll be right back.

We were in a large, busy hospital with many different wards. I had no idea where she'd gone.

Ten minutes later she returned. She placed the cat on the table, dead.

Do you want to be with her? Of course.

The words were out of my mouth before I could stop them: What have you done.

I have heard of a study according to which cats, unlike many other animal species, do not forgive. (Like writers, perhaps, who, according to an editor I know, never forget a slight.)

Maybe the guilt was worse because, of all the cats I'd had, this one had been my least favorite, the one who always remained aloof, the one who would not let me cuddle her or hold her on my lap but who waited till I was asleep before sneaking onto my hip. Now she became the one I could not stop thinking about. I would find a cat hair or whisker somewhere in the apartment and hear again the hoarse, frantic mewing of her last days. No, I did not want another cat. I did not want ever again to watch another cat die, suffer and die. Not to mention that other anxiety: If I did get a cat, what would happen to it if I died first?

Thus was I saved, perhaps, from becoming an old cat lady. I am glad that, in the age of the internet, which has revived the ancient worship of cats as gods, the label is losing its stigma. I was once told by a medical resident that he'd been taught on his psychiatric rotation that owning multiple cats could be a sign of mental illness. Thinking of the horrific instances of animal hoarding I'd heard about, I thought it was good that the psychiatric profession had its ear to this particular ground. But when I asked him *how many* cats were said to put a person over the line, he said *three*.

Given a dog's extraordinary powers of smell, I know that, even though it's been years, Apollo is aware that this house was once feline territory. I want to know: What does he think about that?

There is a Hungarian film called *White God*, in which the dogs of Budapest rise up against the oppressor. Like all uprisings, this one has a leader. This is Hagen, the beloved mixed-breed pet of a girl named Lili. His ordeals begin when Lili's father refuses to pay the tax imposed on anyone in possession of a dog that isn't a purebred. Thrown out in the street, Hagen tries to find his way back to Lili (who meanwhile is doing all she can to find him), but is thwarted, first by dogcatchers, then by a brute who, using the cruelest methods, trains Hagen to fight. It is after he's killed another dog, Hagen's first time in the ring, that he understands not only what he's done but what has been done to him. He escapes his trainer but is soon trapped by dogcatchers and hauled off to the pound, where he is slated to be destroyed. But again Hagen escapes, at the same time liberating a large number of other dogs who follow on his heels as he tears through the streets. The pack of running—in some cases attacking—dogs are joined by more dogs, dogs from every corner of the city: Hagen has raised a canine army. One by one his enemies are sought out and viciously killed. By now, though, the once gentle Hagen has been so transformed that when he finally meets Lili again, in the courtyard of the slaughterhouse where her father works as a meat inspector, he bares his teeth and snarls. She is a human being, after all—and her father, who started this war, is there with her. Ranged about Hagen are the members of his army, every one prepared to strike. The frightened Lili remembers how Hagen used to like when she played to him on her horn (her instrument in the school orchestra), and the soothing effect it had on him. She takes the horn from her backpack and begins to play. Hagen is calmed and lies down. Then all the other dogs grow quiet and lie down too. Lili plays on, prolonging the moment of peace.

It is not a happy ending, because we know, of course, that the dogs are doomed. But they have had their revenge.

It's easy to see why many people—including myself, before a high school English teacher set me straight—believe that someone once said, Music soothes the savage beast.

Music has charms to soothe a savage *breast* is what the playwright William Congreve actually wrote. But it's part of our mythology: a wild or angry animal calmed or tamed by music.

Which makes sense, given all we know about how music can affect the spirits of a human being.

In *White God*, right before a dog is put to death, it is placed in a room with a TV showing the old Tom and Jerry cartoon *The Cat Concerto*, in which Tom plays Liszt's Hungarian Rhapsody No. 2.

I don't know if playing music really can soothe a dog's breast, but on the internet I find it among suggestions for dealing with canine depression.

(Are you writing a book? Are you depressed? Are you looking for a pet? Is your pet depressed?)

But what kind of music?

I once had a rabbit that I let run loose in the house. In the living room was a stereo whose two large speakers sat on the floor. Whenever music was put on, the rabbit would make his way to a speaker and plant himself there. Usually he'd just lie still, listening, or maybe he'd start to groom his ears. But if I played Bach's "Sheep May Safely Graze," he would get up and cavort around the room.

What kind of music? Cheerful? Mellow? Fast, or slow? The Hungarian Rhapsody No. 2? How about some Schubert? (Oh, maybe not Schubert, whose pen, in the words of Arvo Pärt, was fifty percent ink, fifty percent tears.) How about Miles Davis's *Bitches Brew*? (I know this is all moronically anthropomorphic, but sometimes that is the form love takes.)

I play him Miles Davis. I play him Bach and Arvo Pärt. I

play him Prince, Adele, and Frank Sinatra. And Mozart, lots of Mozart.

None of which appears to affect him at all. I don't think he's listening. If he is, I don't think he cares.

Then I remember reading about an experiment in which a group of monkeys that were given a choice between listening to Mozart and listening to rock and roll chose Mozart, but when given a choice between Mozart and silence chose silence.

White God was inspired partly by the novel *Disgrace*. After losing his teaching position, David Lurie abandons his life in Cape Town. He retreats to a village on the Eastern Cape where his daughter Lucy has a small subsistence farm, and where he will end up working at an animal shelter. On the fate of the multitude of unwanted dogs, Lucy reflects: They do us the honor of treating us like gods, and we respond by treating them like things.

A letter from my building's management office saying that it has been brought to their attention that I am in violation of my lease. The dog must be removed from the premises immediately, or—

Does something bad happen to the dog?

PART SIX

The problem with this story, a student I'll call Carter says about a story by a student I'll call Jane, is that the protagonist isn't like a character in a story. She's more like a person in real life.

Twice, he says it, because my mind has wandered, and I have to ask him to repeat himself.

You're saying the character is too real? I ask, though I know this is what Carter is saying.

The character in question is a girl with red hair and green eyes who bonds with a girl with blond hair and blue eyes only to discover that the guy the blonde has just dumped is the same person as the redhead's new boyfriend. The color of the boyfriend's eyes and hair are not specified, but he is described as tall. Later, another student, whom I'll call Viv, will say she wants to know if the girlfriend is also tall. Why is that important? I ask, masking my exasperation (as much cannot be said for Viv, who hates being asked to explain anything and replies testily, Can't I just ask?).

There are things I'd like to know too. For example, why, when these two girls want to talk, do they keep getting into their cars and driving to each other's houses? Why do they never use their phones, not even to text to find out first if the other one is home? Why do they not know things about each other that they could easily have learned from Facebook?

It is one of the great bafflements of student fiction. I have read that college students can spend up to ten hours a day on social media. But for the people they write about—also mostly college students—the internet barely exists.

Cell phones do not belong in fiction, an editor once scolded in the margin of one of my manuscripts, and ever since—more than two decades now—I have wondered at the disconnect between tech-filled life and techless story.

If anyone could shed light on the matter, I once thought, it would be the students. But they have not been much help. The most interesting response came from a grad student who happened to be the mother of a five-year-old. Whenever she reads him a story, she said, her son keeps interrupting: When do they go to the bathroom? Mommy, when do they go to the bathroom?

There are things we do all the time in real life that we don't put in our stories: point taken. But no one spends ten hours a day going to the bathroom.

Think of Kurt Vonnegut's complaint that novels that leave out technology misrepresent life as badly as Victorians misrepresented life by leaving out sex.

But that is another mystery. *Nothing in their heads and nothing between their legs* is how one teacher I know describes the characters in workshop stories. This teacher is someone who's been at it much longer than I have and is about to retire. He tells me it wasn't always so.

I remember when there was plenty of sex, he says, a lot of it pretty kinky. Now everyone's afraid of offending someone, triggering something. We should be grateful, though. Nowadays you could get in trouble for discussing sex in class.

I know another man, a teacher at an all-women's college, who got in trouble for including Your First Sexual Experience on a list of suggested writing prompts, prompting some women to file a complaint. According to the dean, what the teacher had done could be—well, had been—considered a form of sexual harassment.

I have taken my school's required online course, Sexual Misconduct Training, and had my eyes opened to the fact that any oral or written reference to sexual behavior including suggestive jokes or cartoons, or casual conversation about one's own or any other person's sex life, comes under the heading Sexual Misconduct. There did not seem to be any exception for a writing workshop. I worried about having assigned a story that included a scene of autoerotic asphyxiation, but it went right over my students' heads. I enlightened them, then worried that perhaps I should not have done that.

Though I confess I only skimmed most of the course material, I was surprised when I came to the final Test Your Knowledge part ("No one will see the results except the test taker"), and got two of the ten questions wrong. It was suggested that I go back and read the relevant sections again, more carefully. But why bother, since I now knew that, yes, I *was* required to report immediately any knowledge I might have of a teacher dating a student, and that although *not* required I was *strongly advised* to report a colleague for telling an off-color joke, even if the joke didn't personally offend me.

What I'm saying, says Carter, is that I know this girl. I can tell you exactly what she looks like.

How's that? The only thing I could tell you about what this girl looks like is what Jane has stated: color of eyes, color of hair—the usual student way of describing a character, as if a story is a piece of ID like a driver's license. So common is this that I've come to think the students must feel that saying too much about a character is rude, an invasion of privacy, and that it's best to be as discreet—that is, nondescript—as possible. A student writing about Carter, for example, would put in that his eyes are brown but leave out the tattoo of barbed wire circling his neck, or the way he keeps rubbing the wrist that is sore from hours of making espresso drinks at the campus Starbucks. They would mention his curly brown hair but not that it is almost always, no matter how warm the day, covered by a black watch cap. They would probably even leave out the silver-dollar-sized ear gauges, which I can never look at without wincing.

I can tell you everything about her, Carter says.

To me, the main character is as thin and gray as this strand of hair I just brushed from my sleeve. But to Carter, the problem is not that she's too vague, but that she's all too familiar.

It is his perennial critique: What's the point in writing stories about the kind of people you meet every day in real life?

Dangerous, Flannery O'Connor called letting students criticize one another's manuscripts: the blind leading the blind.

Carter's own literary ambition is to be the next George R. R. Martin. His novel in progress depicts epic clashes between imaginary kingdoms waging never-ending war in pursuit of power, dominance, and revenge. Unlike his idol, though, he can't be taken to task for scenes of sexual violence. There is no rape or incest in his pages. There is no sex at all, and women are hardly mentioned. When people in class express doubts about a novel that doesn't include any significant female characters, Carter shrugs and says nothing. But alone in my office he tells me that, in fact, there are women in his novel. And there is sex, he says. Loads of it. Most of it violent. There is rape. There is gang rape. There is incest.

I delete all that for the workshop, he says.

He rolls his eyes when I ask him why.

Are you kidding? You know how people would react. I mean, like, the women? I could get kicked out of school.

When I say I'm sure no such thing would happen, he is not convinced. Today he is wearing his black watch cap (oh what is he watching?) low on his brow, which gives him a Cro-Magnon look. His stretched lobes make his ears resemble the floppy ears of one of his fictional half-humans.

Well, I'm not taking any chances, he says. But trust me, it's all in there. All the rough stuff, he adds. Which triggers something in me. Which he notices.

But if *you* wanted to see it, he says, I'd show you.

I don't think that's necessary, I stammer, and he gives me a knowing smirk.

Most of my students do it. Some of my fellow teachers do it. People who work in publishing do it. All are more likely to do it if the writer is a woman. But when did it start, this habit of referring to writers you've never met by first name.

A book festival event in Brooklyn. I catch the 2 train at Fourteenth Street. The car is full. I see two middle-aged people, a man and a woman, seated near me, but not close enough for me to hear their conversation. Body language suggests that they are friends, or colleagues, rather than a couple. Something tells me they are on their way to the same place I am. A half hour later, at Atlantic Avenue, they get off with me. It's a Saturday night, the huge station is packed, I soon lose sight of them. The event is in a hall several blocks from the station. When I get there I go straight to the bar, and there they are, the man and woman from the 2 train, in line just ahead of me.

This semester I share an office with another teacher. She is a new hire, in fact this is her first time teaching. As it happens, only a few years ago this young woman was a student of mine. Same program, same school.

She sometimes does meditation in the office, and the air is suffused with the mimosa or orange-blossom scent of the candles she burns.

Because we teach on different days we don't usually see each other, but we keep in touch through messages and notes, and she sometimes thoughtfully leaves me a treat, a cookie or a chocolate bar or a packet of smoked almonds. Once, for my birthday, she filled the office with flowers.

While she was still a student this woman achieved quite a coup, selling her MFA thesis, a first novel, before it was half finished, along with a second novel before it was even a gleam in her eye. Even before the first book was published she began winning prizes, and after receiving, in quick succession, every literary prize that exists for outstanding promise—a total of almost half a million dollars—she began to be known among us as O.P.

As expected, when it was published, the first novel received excellent reviews. But in spite of this, and in spite of its picking up yet another literary prize, the book did not sell. In our small world O.P. remains famous, she is "that girl who gets everything." But in the wider world, even among those who pay attention to new fiction, two years after its debut neither the book's name nor the author's is likely to ring a bell.

Hardly a new story, and hardly the end of the world. But try telling O.P., who for two years now hasn't been able to write at all.

She had thought teaching might help, or at least give her something useful to do. As a student, though introverted, she had radiated confidence. But as a teacher she is overwhelmed. She is about the same age as most of her students and even younger than some. She is fully aware how her inexperience shows, how lacking she is in projecting authority. She has a high, thin, naturally quavery voice and a tendency, when anxious, to flush.

She is bitter about her female students, who she senses have it in for her, and from whom she constantly gets the who-do-you-think-you-are vibe women often give off to other women, in particular striving and ambitious women. Among the male students, three have already come on to her. One is so successful at undressing her with his eyes that she finds herself sitting in class with her arms crossed over her breasts. Worse, she finds herself intensely attracted to him.

She sometimes has panic attacks before class. Hence the meditation, sometimes supplemented with benzodiazepine.

O.P. is tormented by the fear not only that she'll never write again but that her whole life is a lie. Everything she has accomplished so far has been the result of some mistake. Why anyone had wanted to publish her—why anyone thought she could teach—baffling! As for that second novel, no matter how many extensions the publisher grants, she knows she'll never pull it off.

O.P. lives in terror of being exposed: she is not just a failure, she is a fraud. *And would everyone please stop calling her O.P.!*

Useless to remind her that identical doubts have bedeviled other writers for all time, including, and perhaps even especially, some of the greatest. Useless to quote Kafka on *The Metamorphosis*: "Imperfect almost to its very marrow."

Another teacher, who's at school on the same days as O.P., reports sometimes hearing her weeping behind her closed door, once because she was hopelessly struggling to write a simple two-page student thesis report.

The day I sit in on one of her classes for a required department observation, I see how the student to whom she has confessed being attracted gazes at her with a tenderly gloating expression. I do not put in my observation report what I believe is the case, that she has started having an affair with this student. If I'm lucky she won't confide in me, she won't seek my advice.

I can see this happening one day: I'll be in a certain place, maybe a store that sells beauty products, or some kind of salon, or the bathroom of a home where I happen to be a guest. I'll get a whiff of a particular scent, mimosa or orange blossom, but I won't remember the candles O.P. used to burn in our office, and so I'll be bewildered by my response: a tremor of alarm, as if I'd just telepathically learned that someone I know is in trouble.

Across from the office I share with O.P. is the office of this year's Distinguished Visiting Writer, but he is never there. He does not hold office hours and has instructed the program secretary to forward mail to his home rather than use his school mail slot. When he comes in to teach he goes straight to his workshop classroom. Few of his colleagues ever cross paths with him, and when they do he looks right through the person as if they're not there. Before the semester began he instructed the chair to inform faculty that he does not do book blurbs. He himself informed students on the first day of class: I don't do letters of recommendation. *Don't even ask.*

When you heard this, you were indignant: I should've told *him* that back when he asked me to write him a letter for the Guggenheim.

Soon after the semester begins, he gives a reading at a Barnes & Noble. The fact that the audience is sparse does not discourage him; he reads for the good part of an hour.

During the Q&A, when someone asks why his book, whose

form is highly unconventional, is called a novel, he responds, It's a novel because I say it is.

During the signing, a woman urges him to write another book as quickly as possible. Because, you know, she says earnestly, there's nothing out there.

In Barnes & Noble.

In the news: Thirty-two million adult Americans can't read. The potential audience for poetry has shrunk by two-thirds since 1992. A "rent-burdened" woman worrying how she's going to survive in New York City decides to try writing a novel ("and that's going well").

PART SEVEN

Wife One lives abroad. She had flown to New York for the memorial event, and one night before she flew home she and I went out to dinner.

"I know it's worse for you," she said kindly. "We were married, but that was so long ago. And after it was over, nothing. No friendship, no contact, nothing. That's how it had to be. And I'll be honest, at first I thought I wouldn't even go to the memorial. But then I thought, you know, closure. Whatever that means."

When it's suicide, someone at the memorial said, there can be no closure.

"But you," she said. "You two were such good friends for so long. How I used to envy that. I used to think, if only he and I hadn't fallen in love, then *we* could have had a friendship like that!"

But there'd been no resisting, had there. A love so potent it might have been the effect of a spell. One of those grand passions given only to some to experience, the rest to hear tell and dream about.

Even now it has the force of legend for me: beautiful, terrible, doomed.

I remember when being near the two of you was like being near a furnace. And I remember thinking, when things went wrong, that one or the other of you was going to end up dead. You yourself said it sometimes felt like you were doing something forbidden, even criminal. And she, raised Catholic, was convinced that such idolizing love had to be a sin. And, of course, in the end it was this that drove Wife Two to despair: not all your womanizing but the belief that such love doesn't come twice in a life, that whatever you felt for her could not equal what you'd felt for Wife One, who, she would always fear, still had your heart.

If only we hadn't fallen in love: she said it over and over.

"I was just thinking about it on the cab ride here. Remember how we worshipped him? How we were all his little groupies? What did they call us back then?"

"A literary Manson family."

"Oh God, yes. Ugh. How could I forget."

Remember how we hung on your every word and ran out and bought every book or album you mentioned.

Remember how everything we wrote was some pathetic imitation of you.

Remember how you had us believing that one day you'd win the Nobel Prize.

Now he's just another dead white male.

He did all right, I said. He did better than most writers.

"But I hear the last couple of years he didn't write much."

No.

"Did he seem that depressed? Did he talk about it? I'm not just asking, it's been keeping me up nights. Why did he quit teaching?"

I recite your various gripes, which were not much different from those heard every day from other teachers: how even students from top schools didn't know a good sentence from a bad one, how nobody in publishing seemed to care how anything was written anymore, how books were dying, literature was dying, and the prestige of the writer had sunk so low that the biggest mystery of all was why everyone and their grandmother was turning to authorship as just the ticket to glory.

I tell her about your loss of conviction in the purpose of fiction—today, when no novel, no matter how brilliantly written or full of ideas, was going to have any meaningful effect on society, when it was impossible even to imagine anything like what had led Abraham Lincoln to say, meeting Harriet Beecher Stowe, in 1862, So you're the little woman who wrote the book that started this great war.

If Abraham Lincoln really did say that.

That's when I remember the interview.

How strange to have forgotten it, even for a time. The interview, which it now occurs to me was probably your last, for the inaugural issue of a midwestern literary journal.

The interview in which you made a prediction that there would be a wave of suicides among writers.

And when do you see this happening?

Soon.

I remember being surprised that you hadn't mentioned that interview, which I might have missed altogether if another friend hadn't forwarded it to me.

I didn't mention it because I was embarrassed. It occurred to me later how it would sound—melodramatic, self-pitying. I'd had a few drinks.

I remember the interviewer asked the usual question about audience, whether you wrote with a particular reader in mind. Which set you off about the relationship between writer and reader and how much that relationship had changed. As a young writer you'd been told, Never assume your reader isn't as intelligent as you are. Advice you'd taken to heart. You wrote with that reader in mind, you said, someone as smart as—or why not even smarter than!—yourself. Someone intellectually curious, who had the habit of reading, who loved books as much as you did. Who loved fiction. And then, with the internet, had come the possibility of reading the responses of actual readers, among whom you were pleased to find some who did indeed match, more or less, the reader in your head. But there were others—

not just one or two but quite a number when you added them up—who had misread, or misunderstood, in some cases quite seriously, what you'd said. Troubling enough when the reader was someone who'd hated the book, but that was far from always the case. Like other writers, you now found yourself regularly damned or praised for things that had never occurred to you, things you had never expressed and never would express, things that represented pretty much the opposite of what you actually believed.

All this, you said, had thrown you for a loop. Because, although you knew you were supposed to be glad for each and every copy of a book that was sold, and you knew you were supposed to feel grateful for any reader, who after all might have chosen to read any one of millions of other books instead of yours, you honestly found it hard to be happy about a reader who got things all wrong, you honestly would just as soon a reader like that ignore your book and go read something else.

But hasn't it always been this way?

No doubt. But in the past the writer didn't have to know, the problem wasn't right there in your face.

But what about "Trust the tale not the teller," and how the critic's job is to save the work from the writer?

By "critic," you know, Lawrence did not mean self-appointed. I would love to see the consumer review that saved a book from its author.

Well, if I could just play devil's advocate here: Let's say I invite someone to dinner and cook them a fabulous beef stew and they gobble it up and say, Wow, yum, that's the best lamb stew I ever had! So what? Isn't the main thing that they enjoyed it?

Oh, were we talking about dinner? Well, let me say this: I don't take it lightly if when I write the word *beef* someone chooses to read *lamb*. People talking about a book as if it were just another thing, like a dish, or a product like an electronic device or a pair of shoes, to be rated for consumer satisfaction—that was just the goddamn trouble, you said. Even those aspiring writers your students seemed never to judge a book on how well it fulfilled the author's intentions but solely on whether it was the kind of book that they liked. And so you got papers stating things like "I hate Joyce, he's so full of himself," or "I don't see why I should have to read about white people problems." You got customer reviews full of umbrage, suggesting that if a book didn't affirm what the reader already felt—what they could identify with, what they could relate to—the author had no business writing the book at all. Those hilarious stories that people loved, and loved to share—the book clubber who said, When I read a novel I want someone to die in it; the complaint against Anne Frank's diary, in which nothing much happens and then the story just breaks off—did not make *you* laugh. Oh, you knew that a lot of people, including other writers, would accuse you of being precious. Some would say that, after all, the one sure way for an artist to know his work had failed was if everyone "got" it. But the truth was, you had become so dismayed by the ubiquity of careless reading that something had happened that you had thought never could happen: you had started not to care whether people read you or not. And though you knew your publisher would spit in your eye for saying so, you were inclined to agree with whoever it was who said that no truly good book would find more than three thousand readers.

"Oh dear," says Wife One.

Near the end of the interview, you got on the subject of mentors and teaching and blasted the new rules forbidding romance between professors and students.

What a load of crap, this notion of making the university a safe place. Think of all the wonderful things in life that could never have happened—all the great things that would never have been created or discovered or even imagined—if the top priority had been to make everyone feel *safe*. Who'd want to live in such a world?

"Oh dear, oh dear."

The only part of the interview I hadn't heard before was the part about the suicides.

I'd had a few drinks. I asked to see the interview before it ran and was told yes of course, but then the prick never sent it.

I tell Wife One about the episode with the women students who would not be called *dear*. Something I don't tell her, and which is another thing I'd forgotten but that has just now come back: on the day of the interview you were upset, and you told me why. You suspected that your agent had submitted your last novel to the publisher without having read it.

I'm glad to hear that magazine is folding. It was a shitty little magazine.

"This is what's been keeping me up nights," says Wife One. "Something I read, about how, among people who try to kill themselves and survive, almost all say they regretted it. Like jumpers who say that as soon as they hit the air they knew they'd made a mistake, they didn't really want to die."

I've heard this too, but also another story, from another era, about what coroners supposedly learned from the corpses of people who drowned themselves in, I believe it was, the Seine. Those whose reason for wanting to die was love had tried to scramble back out of the water. Those whose reason was financial ruin had sunk like stones.

Getting old. We know this must have been the hardest thing, much harder for you even than for other people. A man who once could have had any woman he wanted. Who had groupies hanging on his every word and believing he could win the Nobel Prize.

Even if it was just a bunch of silly, infatuated girls like us.

We had begun to draw attention. Two women bent over their entrées, holding hands, dabbing at their eyes with their napkins.

. . .

Later, when she gets her first look at Apollo, on Skype, she says, "Holy shit! I can't believe they dumped a monster like that on you. No wonder no one wants him."

I wince. I cannot bear to hear Apollo called unwanted. I remember Wife Three shrugging off my suggestion that there must be many people who'd want such a beautiful dog: Maybe if he was a puppy.

"And I don't see how he could've expected you to adopt him if it meant losing your home."

"I'm sure either I never told him I couldn't have a dog or he forgot."

"But the fact that he didn't ask, never even ran it by you as if you had no say in the matter. I can't imagine what he was thinking."

But I can. For I have imagined it many times: how, among all the other questions certain to have come to you, was what will happen to the dog.

I know of another suicide, among whose last things was taking her dog to the pound. A farewell that does not bear thinking about.

Not that you put it in writing: like most suicides, you put nothing in writing. Nor did you change anything in the will you had made out years before. But you made sure your wife knew.

She lives alone, she doesn't have a partner or any kids or pets, she works mostly at home, and she loves animals—that's what he said.

Maybe at some point you did consider discussing it with me, maybe you were even planning to do so. But then. Suicides often choose their moment at random, I'm told, in a mood of it's now or never, when even a pause to scribble farewell could mean time to lose one's nerve. (He who hesitates is not lost.)

Maybe you were afraid that if we were actually to have that conversation—what would happen to your dog in the event of your death—I might guess, or at least suspect, what you were contemplating.

When I tell Wife One how old Apollo is, a senior dog of a short-lived breed that the vet gave maybe two more years, she says, "That makes it even worse. Maybe if he was a puppy I could understand. But what are you supposed to do with an old dog that size? How are you going to take care of him if he becomes infirm?"

This thought, with all its dire implications, has of course already occurred to me.

"I don't know," she says. "I feel like there's something mad about this whole situation."

Ah. Since I first heard about your death, haven't I often felt like someone living with one foot in madness. Early on, there were times when I would find myself somewhere without remembering how I got there, when I'd leave home on some errand only to forget what it was. I went to school one day minus the lecture notes I could not teach without. I mixed up doctors' appointments and showed up at the wrong office. Why were the students staring at me? Had I said something nonsensical, or repeated something I'd just said five minutes ago? Or was I imagining that they were staring at all.

A Hallmark sympathy card from the department secretary—hideous, touching—makes me cry for an hour.

By the time Apollo came to live with me such incidents had become less frequent. But there lingers over all the fog of the unreal. At times it's as if I truly am in a fairy tale. When people say, What are you going to do when you get evicted, you can't just sit around waiting for a miracle, I think, But that is what I'm waiting for!

I'm in one of those stories where a person is put to a test, one of those fables where someone encounters a stranger—could be human, could be beast—who is in need of help. If the person refuses to help he is dealt a harsh punishment. If the person is kind to the one in need—often a rich, royal, or powerful being in disguise—he reaps a reward, more often than not the love of the being whose exalted identity has now been revealed.

I like the story of Greta Garbo watching Cocteau's film *Beauty and the Beast*. What she was heard to cry out at the end, when the spell is broken and the Beast appears in the princely form of actor Jean Marais: Give me back my beautiful beast!

Sometimes a dog figures in this kind of story. Like the Islamic tale about a prostitute who brings water to a dog dying of thirst and by this act so pleases God that she is forgiven all her sins and allowed to enter heaven.

"It's not his fault he's not a cute little puppy. It's not his fault he's so big. And it might sound crazy, but I have this feeling that if I don't keep him something bad will happen. If he has to move one more time, he could develop so many problems he'll end up having to be put down. And I can't let that happen. I have to save him."

Wife One says, "Who are we talking about."

Is this the madness at the heart of it? Do I believe that if I am good to him, if I act selflessly and make sacrifices for him, do I believe that if I love Apollo—beautiful, aging, melancholy Apollo—I will wake one morning to find him gone and you in his place, back from the land of the dead?

———

Now that Hector has reported me to the landlord he feels bad. Whenever he sees me he looks abashed.

I'm sorry, he says, but you know, you know—

I know you had to do your job.

He's a good dog, he says.

He seems touched that Apollo allows his head to be stroked, as if he thinks Apollo must know what Hector has done.

You have a place to go?

Not yet, but something will turn up, I tell him with a blitheness I don't have to fake: my life has become so unreal that I barely skimmed the second notice from the building management office before throwing it away.

It's a shame, Hector says. Such a beautiful animal. I'm very sorry.

It's not your fault.

To prove that I don't blame him, I plan to give him a bigger tip this Christmas than I gave him last year.

I can't tell for sure whether Apollo likes to be massaged or is just tolerating it. But I keep it up, getting him to lie first on one side then on the other, pausing for a chest rub in between. The chest rub is what he seems to like best. He doesn't like having his paws touched, though the brat in me keeps trying.

He has grown used to his new home, and to me. Except when I have to be at school, I don't leave him alone. Apart, he is always on my mind and I am anxious to get back to him. He greets me at the door (has he been by the door the whole time?), but with a drowning look that says it hasn't been easy, the waiting. (How good is his memory? If very good, as dogs' memories are said to be, what grief being locked up alone might bring him. And—heart-shredding thought—is it still for *you* that he waits by the door?)

His tail moves side to side, a wag for sure, but a wistful one. Never happy tail, the furious whipping back and forth for which Great Danes are known (to the extent that injuries to the tail and damage to household objects are common: the reason many owners choose docking).

The air mattress is back in the closet. Not end of story. He has never again growled at me, and when I say *Down* I don't usually have to say it twice. Still, the bed is where he wants to be, especially at night. (I tried getting him to consider the air mattress a dog bed but it didn't work.) Despite what the vet had said, I didn't see the necessity of banishing him from the bed completely. After all, plenty of people allow their dogs on the bed. Some even place a special blanket at the foot of the bed for the dog to sleep on. If Apollo was a toy poodle curled up on a special blanket at the foot of the bed, it would be nothing extraordinary. Why is it different when the dog is the size of a man and stretched out with his head on his own pillow? I acknowledge that it is. But let me say this: When you're lying in bed full of night thoughts, such as why did your friend have to die and how much longer will it be before you lose the roof over your head, having a huge warm body pressed along the length of your spine is an amazing comfort.

He knows all the commands.

One night after a long bad day—lost cell phone, listless class, failed attempt to get back to writing—Apollo stirs, starts leaving the bed, and I find myself saying, *Stay.*

Certain friends, I've noticed, are avoiding me, I can't help thinking at least partly because they're afraid some day soon I'll show up at their door with Apollo and a suitcase.

. . .

The friend who is most sympathetic about my situation calls to ask how I am. I tell him about trying music and massage to treat Apollo's depression, and he asks if I've considered a therapist. I tell him I'm skeptical about pet shrinks, and he says, That's not what I meant.

End of semester. I tell my family I can't travel to be with them this Christmas. During the monthlong break before teaching resumes, I'll hardly ever have to be apart from Apollo. Even in coldest weather, we go out and we walk and walk. We like cold weather. We like the city in winter. More room on the sidewalks. Fewer gawkers. And when it's freezing Apollo isn't as likely to stop for one of his rests.

Final warning from the building management office. It occurs to me I might try talking to the landlord. Who's to say the man's a heartless prick and not the very soul of compassion? Why not a Christmas miracle! At the very least I could beg him for time.

I call the managing agent and ask for the landlord's number in Florida.

We don't give out that number, he says.

Twelve authors—six men and six women—have posed nude for a photo wall calendar. The email invitation urges me not to miss this exclusive offer: a limited edition of copies signed by each author now available for presale.

Jolted to recall a panel discussion at which someone raised the topic of dignity and its diminished place in the literary world. Watch, you said, it'll be nude author photos next. How you sat with a face of stone while everyone else in the room laughed.

New Year's Eve. I stay home and watch, hardly for the first time, *It's a Wonderful Life.* I don't open the bottle of champagne that a student has sent to thank me for writing a letter of recommendation for the thirty-plus MFA programs she is applying to this year.

The friend who is most sympathetic about my situation organizes an intervention. The following week: a barrage of calls and messages from various people, some of whom I haven't heard from in years.

They don't want to see me lose my home. They want me to come to my senses before it's too late. I need a better way to cope with my feelings of loss and guilt. I need bereavement therapy. Here are some names. I should think about medication. Here's what worked for them. There are books. There are websites. There are support groups. Healing won't come from withdrawing into a fantasy world, isolating myself, spending all my time with a dog. There is such a thing as pathological grief. There is the magical thinking of pathological grief, which is a kind of dementia. Which in their collective opinion is what I have.

Generous offers of all kinds are made, though no one volunteers to take the dog.

Then Wife Two, of all people, does just that: I have a little grandson who adores dogs. He'll be thrilled with one big enough to ride.

That would have solved everything, says Wife One.

I say you would never forgive me. And was it not suspicious, Wife Two even making such an offer.

"What do you mean? I thought she was just trying to help."

"Help? This woman who's always hated me, almost as much as she hates you. I would never trust her. Just remember what that marriage was like: all rage and bitterness and resentment. I wouldn't trust Apollo anywhere near her."

Women are dangerous, they stop at nothing and they never let go.

Wife One thinks I'm being paranoid. But in fact it's far from unheard of: people taking out their revenge against some person on that person's helpless child or pet.

You would never forgive me.

"So what are you going to do? You can't just sit around waiting for a miracle."

But that is what I am waiting for.

PART EIGHT

Advice often given to writers: read your drafts out loud. Advice I am usually too lazy to follow. But I will try anything these days that might keep me longer at my desk. I pick up the pages I've just printed out and start reading. Behind me I hear Apollo, who has been sleeping behind the couch, heave himself to his feet. He trots to the desk (we are about eye to eye when I'm sitting) and stares at me as if I'm doing something remarkable. Or maybe, though we've had one long walk already today, he wants to go out again.

When I reach the bottom of the page I pause, thinking. Apollo pokes me with his nose. He barks, very low, just once. He takes a step forward, a step to the right, a step back, all the while cocking his head from side to side: his way of saying WTF.

He wants me to keep reading! True or not, that's what I do. But soon I stop.

Read your sentences out loud, goes the advice, and you'll hear what doesn't sound right, what doesn't work. I hear, I hear. What doesn't sound right, what doesn't work. *I hear.*

No different from when I read the sentences to myself.

I fold my arms on the desk and hide my face in them.

Poke. *Woof.* I turn my head. Apollo's gaze is deep, his mismatched ears look sharp as razors. He licks my face and does the cha-cha thing again. He wags his tail, and for the thousandth time I think how frustrating it must be for a dog: the endless trouble of making yourself understood to a human.

I move from chair to couch, Apollo watching, forehead creased. Once I'm settled, he comes and sits down in front of me. Eye to eye. What do dogs think when they see someone cry? Bred to be comforters, they comfort us. But how puzzling human unhappiness must be to them. We who can fill our dishes any time and with as much food as we like, who can go outside whenever we wish, and run free—we who have no master constantly needing to be pleased, or obeyed—WTF?

From the stack of books on the coffee table, I pick up Rilke's *Letters to a Young Poet*, an assigned book for one of my courses. I open it and start reading out loud. After a few pages Apollo assumes the half-open-mouthed smile seen all the time on other dogs' faces but with worrying infrequency on his. As I keep reading he lowers himself to the floor, covering my feet and pressing against my shins. He relaxes his head onto his paws, tipping his eyes at me each time I turn a page. The position of his ears shifts in response to my vocal inflections. I am reminded of my pet rabbit hunched by the stereo speaker. But Apollo never appeared to enjoy the music I played for him, was never soothed—not by music, not by massage—as he appears to be soothed now.

So I read on—as clearly and with as much expression as I would to someone who could understand every word. And I too find it soothing: the lyrical prose in my mouth, the great warm gently heaving weight on my legs and feet.

I know this little book well: ten letters addressed to a student who'd written to ask Rilke for advice when Rilke himself was just twenty-seven years old. Letter eight contains his famous vision of the Beauty and the Beast myth: *Perhaps all the dragons in our lives are princesses who are only waiting to see us act, just once, with beauty and courage. Perhaps everything that frightens us is, in its deepest essence, something helpless that wants our love.* Words often quoted, or paraphrased, including recently in an epigraph to the film *White God*: Everything terrible is something that needs our love.

Beware irony, ignore criticism, look to what is simple, study the small and humble things of the world, do what is difficult precisely because it is difficult, do not search for answers but rather love the questions, do not run away from sadness or depression for these might be the very conditions necessary to your work. Seek solitude, above all seek solitude.

I have read Rilke's advice so often I know it by heart.

When I read the letters for the first time—at around the same age as Rilke when he wrote them—I felt that they had been written as much to me as to their addressee, that all this wonderful advice was meant for any person who wished to become a writer.

But now, though the writing might strike me as more beautiful than ever, I cannot read it without uneasiness. I cannot forget my own students, who do not feel at all what the Young Poet must have felt when he received them in the first decade of the last century. They do not feel what we felt when you assigned this book to us, three-quarters of a century later, along with Rilke's autobiographical novel, *The Notebooks of Malte Laurids Brigge*. They do not feel that Rilke is speaking to them. On the contrary: they accuse him of excluding them. They say it's a lie that writing is a religion requiring the devotion of a priest. They say it's ridiculous.

When I tell them the myth about Rilke's death, how it came to be said that the onset of his fatal disease occurred after he pricked his hand on the thorn of a rose—that flower that obsessed him and was such a significant symbol in his work—they groan, and one student can't stop laughing.

There was a time when young writers—at least the ones we knew—believed that Rilke's world was eternal. I agree with my students that that world has vanished. But at their age it would not have occurred to me that it *could* vanish, let alone in my lifetime.

Nothing brings more anxiety than Rilke's avowal that a person who feels he can live without writing shouldn't be writing at all. *Must* I write? is the question he commands the student to ask himself *in the most silent hour of your night.* If you were forbidden to write, would you die? (Words taken to heart by Lady Gaga, or at least to biceps, which is where she had them, in their original German, tattooed.)

We must love one another or die is how another poet once ended a stanza of what was to become one of the world's most famous poems. But the author of "September 1, 1939" came to despise that poem and was so bothered by the obvious falsehood in that particular line that, before allowing the poem to be reprinted in an anthology, he insisted it be revised: We must love one another *and* die. And later still, qualmish still, correction notwithstanding, he renounced the whole poem—irremediably corrupted, to his mind—altogether.

I think of this story about Auden.

I think about how there was a time when you and I believed that writing was the best thing we could ever hope to do with our lives. (*The best vocation in the world.* Natalia Ginzburg.)

I think about how you had started telling your students that if there was anything else they could do with their lives instead of becoming writers, any other profession, they should do it.

It was around this time last year: I was cleaning out closets. From a top shelf I pulled down boxes of photographs and clippings and papers, among them your old letters. I had forgotten how many there were, from those days before email.

It seems that I was often seeking advice.

You want to know what you should write about. You're afraid that whatever you write will be trivial, or just another version of something that's already been said. But remember, there is at least one book in you that cannot be written by anyone else but you. My advice is to dig deep and find it.

He too left trails of weeping women. But of the two types of womanizer, most definitely the kind that loves women. It was only women, Rilke said, that he could talk to. Only women that he could understand and be himself around (so long as he didn't have to be around too long). And few men have found so many women willing to love, protect, and forgive them.

Once again I come upon his famous definition of love: *two solitudes that protect and border and greet each other.*

What does that even mean? writes a student in her final paper. It's just *words*. It has nothing to do with *real life*, which is where love *actually happens*.

The exasperated, hostile tone so often to be found in student papers.

In real life, he could not be a husband to his wife, whom he left about a year after their marriage. He could not be a father to his daughter. Rilke, who found such richness and meaning in the experience of childhood, and who wrote so many beautiful words about children, neglected his only child. Which did not stop her from dedicating her life to his work and his memory. Then, aged seventy-one, she killed herself.

Rilke, who loved dogs and looked hard at them and shared a boundless communion with them. Who once found in the imploring look of an ugly, heavily pregnant stray that he encountered outside a café in Spain *everything that probes beyond the solitary soul and goes God knows where—into the future or into that which passeth understanding.* He fed her the lump of sugar from his coffee, which, he later wrote, was like reading mass together.

Rilke, in whose work Apollo is a recurring figure.

The book is short, it can be read aloud in about two hours. But soon Apollo has dropped off, like a child at whose bedside a mother has been reading and waiting for precisely this moment to tiptoe away. I'm not tiptoeing anywhere. Pinned beneath his weight, my feet have gone numb. I wiggle them and he wakes. Without getting up he seeks my hand, still holding the little book, and he licks it.

Now we are both up, heading for the kitchen. I pour him some kibble—it's that time—and while he eats I get ready to take him out.

I might have dismissed the incident as something out of my anthropomorphic fancy, but the very next day this happens: I'm sitting on the couch with my laptop when Apollo comes up and starts sniffing the books on the coffee table. His giant jaws open and close around the new paperback copy of the Knausgaard book that I bought to replace the one he destroyed. Oh, not *again*! But before I can take it away, he gently places the book by my side.

I've heard of therapy dogs, of course. Dogs trained to work in hospitals, nursing homes, disaster areas, and the like, their purpose to bring comfort and cheer in hopes of lightening whatever suffering humans might be going through. I know such dogs have been around a long time, also that they are now often used to help children with emotional or learning difficulties. To improve speech and literacy skills, children in schools and libraries are being encouraged to read aloud to dogs. Excellent results have been reported, with children who read to dogs said to progress significantly better than children who read to other humans. Many of the listeners are said to appear to enjoy themselves, showing signs of alertness and curiosity. But an analysis of the full benefits to canines of being read to by humans is not something my research turns up.

It occurs to me that someone used to read to Apollo. Not that I think he was a trained certified therapy dog. (Would such a valuable animal end up a stray?) But I believe that someone must have read aloud to him—or if not *to* him at least while he was present—and that his memory of that experience is a happy one. Maybe it was just that whoever did the reading was someone he loved. (Was it you? Not to her knowledge, says Wife Three. Never in her presence, at any rate.) Or maybe, though not a professional therapy dog, Apollo had nevertheless been expected to help someone by listening to that person read, a responsibility he took seriously and for which he was praised and rewarded. It's in the nature of many dogs to do some kind of work, training manuals say (*assigned a task, dogs showing signs of boredom or depression often perk up*), but people almost never give them enough—if anything—to do.

Or maybe Apollo is a canine genius who has figured something out about me and books. Maybe he understands that, when I'm not feeling so great, losing myself in a book is the best thing I could do. Maybe this is something his phenomenal nose tells him. If, as studies show, a dog's nose is capable of detecting cancer, it would not be surprising if it could also detect changes caused by the relief of stress, or by the experience of mental stimulation or pleasure. If some dogs can predict seizures in people, as we know has occurred, how strange would it be for one to predict a looming fit of the blues?

In fact, the more I live with Apollo, the more convinced I am that Grumpy Vet was right: we humans don't know the half of how dogs' brains work. They may well, in their mute, unfathomable way, know us better than we know them. In any case, the image is irresistible: an avalanche of despair and, like the Saint Bernard coming through the snow with a mini barrel of brandy, Apollo fetches a book.

Even if we know Saint Bernards never really did that.

There was a time when it would have been clearer to me whether reading Rilke's letters to a young poet to a dog was a sign of mental unbalance.

I decide to make reading aloud part of our routine. Knowing how this might look to others, though, I don't tell anyone. But then there's a lot in these pages I've never told anyone.

It is curious how the act of writing leads to confession.

Not that it doesn't also lead to lying your head off.

Like Rilke, Flannery O'Connor wrote a series of letters to a stranger who wrote to her one day out of the blue. In the collection of O'Connor's letters published after her death, this particular correspondent, who'd asked to remain anonymous, is called A. At thirty-two she is two years older than O'Connor, who is nevertheless more than up to shouldering the role of mentor. The letters to A., written over a period of nine years, are filled with thoughts about literature and religion and what it means to be a writer and a believer in the Catholic Church. She talks freely about her fiction writing, and when A. sends her some of her own fiction the response is encouraging. A. has a gift for story writing, O'Connor says, judging one particular story to be "just about perfect." When A. appears to be suffering from a block, O'Connor is quick to blame the devil. For the serious Catholic O'Connor, the devil is not a metaphor.

Though in time the two women arrange to meet, they will not do so often. Meanwhile, on paper, the friendship thrives, bringing them close enough for O'Connor to call A. her "adopted kin." Overjoyed when A. decides to join the Church, she agrees to be her confirmation sponsor.

But in the end the devil won. A. loses her faith. She leaves the Church. Though she produces work in several genres, she publishes nothing. At seventy-five, thirty-four years after O'Connor's death from lupus at the age of thirty-nine, Hazel Elizabeth Hester, known as Betty, shoots herself to death.

If O'Connor had been my mentor, if she'd been writing to me, I might have asked her this: What exactly did Simone Weil mean when she said, When you have to make a decision in life, about what you should do, do what will cost you the most.

Do what is difficult because it is difficult. Do what will cost you the most. Who *were* these people?

If writing *wasn't* painful, O'Connor says, it would not be worth doing.

Turn then to Virginia Woolf, who said that putting feelings into words *takes the pain away*. Making a scene come right, making a character come together: there was no greater pleasure, she said.

———

First faculty meeting of the semester. Should students be allowed to read assigned books on their cell phones. The majority is firm: other electronic devices, okay, but for God's sake not cell phones. But where's the logic, argues O.P. If all we're talking about is screen size. Isn't that like saying they can't read printed books in pocket editions? No, that's different, the majority agrees. Though fifteen minutes later no one has succeeded in articulating exactly how so.

Office hours. Student A is frustrated that the program requires so many reading courses: I don't want to read what other people write, I want people to read what I write. Student B is concerned that so much of the assigned reading includes books that failed to make money or are now out of print. Shouldn't we be studying more successful writers?

It happens fairly often: I hear from a former student that she's had a baby. The book she'd been working on has had to be put aside. Maybe when the child is a little older she can get back to it, she says. Then, when the child is a little older—usually around two—she has another baby.

They keep coming. Announcements of opportunities to study writing paired with some other activity. You can write and enjoy gourmet food, write and taste wines, write and hike in the mountains, write and sail on a cruise ship, write and lose weight, write and kick your addiction, write and learn to knit, cook, bake, speak French or Italian, et cetera. Today, a flyer for a literary festival: *Who says writing and relaxation don't mix? Enjoy the perfect getaway: a writing workshop spa retreat.* (Mani-Pedi-Story, O.P. quips.)

At the bookstore. A friend's most recent novel, published last year, is now out in paperback. Chagrined to realize that not only have I still not read it, I had forgotten all about it.

At the eye doctor's. A middle-aged woman with dyed-black hair the exact shade of her leather jacket enters the waiting room. I have a familiar feeling about her and almost cry Aha! when I see the logo of *The New York Review of Books* on her tote bag. She sits down and pulls out an issue of—the *London Review of Books.*

Academic joke making the rounds: Professor A: Have you read that book? Professor B: Read it? I haven't even taught it yet.

In the faculty club. Another teacher and I drink gin and amuse ourselves speculating: in the event of a school shooting, which of our students would we or would we not take a bullet for.

.   .   .

Sometimes in the banner, other times in a right-hand window, or waiting, a surprise to be revealed as I scroll down the screen: James Patterson. James Patterson, the bestselling author in the world, who has placed, consecutively, more than twenty times at number one on the *New York Times* bestseller list. Who, apparently of a modesty as vast as his success, believes equal success to be within easy reach of, well, anyone. Or at least anyone possessing ninety dollars for the twenty-two video lessons plus exercises he's offering, thirty-day money-back guarantee. *Stop reading this and start writing.* James Patterson, one of the world's richest authors, net worth $700 million (probably more now). *Focus on the story not the sentence.* His image: elderly, kindly, relaxed. A normal guy, bespectacled, in a dark blue sweater. *Defeat the blank page!* Sometimes shown writing on a legal pad (never a computer). *What are you waiting for? You too can write a bestseller.* James Patterson. Always popping up, urging, coaxing, promising the world. Like the devil.

Are you kidding? says a friend who raises goats on a farm upstate and makes award-winning chèvre. Writer's block was the best thing that ever happened to me.

The anniversary of your death. I want to mark the event but don't know quite how. Not for the first time I go online and watch a video of you giving a reading. I have never seen Apollo respond to a screen, and that includes television (his eyes don't appear to focus on any screen image, not even if it's another dog). If I let him listen, I think he would recognize your voice. What stops me from finding out for sure is the thought that this might be cruel. He may be my dog now (*my dog!*), but I don't believe he's forgotten you. What might hearing your voice do to him? How can he understand? What if he thinks you're trapped inside there?

A story about Judy Garland's children watching *The Wizard of Oz* for the first time. She happened to be away, working abroad, when the children and their nanny sat down to watch the movie, which was playing that day on TV. Though she was well past the age when she'd played Dorothy (sixteen), the children knew their own mother. So that's where she was! Carried off to the witch by the flying monkeys! In an emotional state that does not bear thinking about, the children burst into tears.

In the post office. A young woman accompanied by a spotted mutt enters and gets in line. A clerk behind the counter says, No dogs allowed in here, miss. He's a service dog, the young woman says. That's a service dog? says the clerk. *Yes*, snaps the woman with such fierceness that the clerk responds cautiously. I was just asking, miss. I mean, I don't see any badge or sign. The customer standing in front of the woman turns around, eyes her, eyes the mutt, and turns back, shaking his head. The woman draws herself up. She scalds us all with a look. How dare you. This dog is my emotional support companion. *How dare you question his right to be here.*

What makes this odd scene even odder is that the dog is missing a hind leg.

Watching Apollo sleep. The peaceful rise and fall of his flank. His belly is full, he is warm and dry, he has had a four-mile walk today. As usual when he hunched in the street to do his business I guarded him from passing cars. And, in the park, when a texting jogger bore down on us, Apollo barked and blocked his path before he could run into me. I have played several rounds of tug-of-war with him today, I have talked to him, and sung to him, and read him some poetry. I have trimmed his nails and brushed every inch of his coat. Now, watching him sleep, I feel a surge of contentment. There follows another, deeper feeling, singular and mysterious, yet at the same time perfectly familiar. I don't know why it takes a full minute for me to name it.

What are we, Apollo and I, if not two solitudes that protect and border and greet each other?

It is good to have things settled. Miracle or no miracle, whatever happens, nothing is going to separate us.

PART NINE

Everyone I know is writing a book, the therapist tells me unnecessarily. I meet a lot of writers, and I can tell you writer's block is pretty common.

But I'm not there to talk about writer's block. If I weren't so anxious to be on my way I would explain. Usually when a writer sees that someone else has just published a big piece in a major publication on the very topic they've been working on, they feel dismay. I felt relief. (Well, okay, then, said the editor, sounding relieved himself: I guess you're off the hook.)

To draw me out, the therapist asks what I did for the holidays. When I tell him he says gently (he says everything gently), Sounds like that's one of the ways your loss has affected you: not wanting to be with other people.

Hating to be with other people, I don't say. Terrified of being with other people.

But the truth is, even if I hadn't been worried about leaving Apollo I'd have wanted to be alone.

Strays is what a writer I recently read calls those who, for one reason or another, and despite whatever they might have wanted earlier in life, never really become a part of life, not in the way most people do. They may have serious relationships, they may have friends, even a sizable circle, they may spend large portions of their time in the company of others. But they never marry and they never have children. On holidays, they join some family or other group. This goes on year after year, until they finally find it in themselves to admit that they'd really rather just stay home.

But you must see a lot of people like that, I say to the therapist.

Actually, he says, I don't.

A moment here to retrieve something from the past. For two years when I was in college I earned pocket money working for a couples therapist. The entire job consisted of typing up the transcripts of the therapist's sessions. This was not to help in the treatment of clients but because the therapist was planning to write a book. The couples were mostly middle-aged, and all were married. (The therapist disliked the term *marriage counselor*, calling it fusty.)

Listening to the tapes was often depressing. I remember wondering how the therapist could stand her job, especially after

I learned that, in a high number of cases, the couples were not able even with therapy to reconcile their differences and ended up getting divorced. But this was sometimes the point, said the therapist: to help two people let go.

The therapist herself was strikingly glam, slim and tall and a killer dresser (stiletto boots, cinched sweater dresses), who, at forty, had two divorces behind her. As far as I knew, her clients were kept in the dark about her personal life, but I always wondered whether her marital history might have given at least some of them pause. And I remember thinking that, whatever Tolstoy had to say about unhappy families, unhappy couples were all unhappy in the same way.

Just about every husband had been caught cheating or was suspected of cheating. (More than once it was during a session that a man came clean about his infidelities, and it was during a session that one man confessed to his wife that he was in love with another—man.)

In general the women complained of feeling unwanted, underappreciated, and—apparently worst of all—unlistened to.

The men saw their wives as some version of the Grimms' Fisherman's Wife: always nagging, never content.

Again and again I was struck by the evidence that, for husband and wife, the same word did not always have the same meaning. The same words would come up all the time, and I would type them: *love, sex, marriage, listen, need, help, support, trust, equal, fair, respect, care, share, want, money, work.* I would type the words, and I would listen to the couple talk, and I could tell that the same word meant this to him and that to her. I heard several men object to the use of the word *adultery* to define sleeping with someone outside of the marriage. Adultery is when you make it a habit, insisted one. He doesn't help me, a wife said. And when her husband reeled off a list of errands he'd done for her only that past week: I said *help*! she shrieked. I said *help*!

One other thing I picked up on, listening to all those sessions: the therapist changed her voice slightly depending on whom she was addressing. Always subtle but always there, a difference in pitch or something, hard to describe. Perhaps all in my head. But if I had to, I'd say she was more on the side of the men.

I should have known the therapist would want me to stay for the full hour. When I tell him I've left Apollo tied up outside, he says, Next time, why don't you bring him in?

Next time?

That was the deal. The therapist would give me what I wanted, and in return I'd come back.

At least for a couple more sessions, he says.

Sitting in the therapist's office, Apollo at my side, I can't help smiling. It's like we're in couples therapy.

Except that we get along.

One time, a woman passing us in the street shot me this: Better a dog for a husband than a husband who's a dog, I always say.

Always?

When I was in my twenties, out walking Beau, I sometimes got lewd comments from men. That dog your old man? You sleep with that dog? You fuck that dog, lady? I bet you let him eat you.

I find it unsettling when another woman in the street calls Apollo sexy and tells me she's jealous. You're a lucky, lucky woman, she says.

When the certificate arrives, I waft it under Apollo's nose before sticking it under a magnet on the refrigerator door.

You do realize, says Wife One, that you're committing fraud. Even if it is for a good cause.

I am aware of the righteous anger of those in genuine need of animal support toward the growing number of people passing off ordinary—and in some cases exotic—pets as service animals. I've heard about the skunk in the college dorm, the iguana in the restaurant, the pig on the airplane. I promise that I will not take Apollo anywhere he would not normally be allowed. After making a copy of the certificate to send to the building management agent, I will leave it and the badge from the National Service Animal Registry at home.

As for the therapist, he had no reservations about putting in writing that I was suffering from depression and anxiety aggravated by bereavement, that the dog was providing essential emotional support the loss of which was likely to cause harm to my mental health and might even be life threatening.

Wife One thinks it's funny: Because the truth is, in this case it's the animal who can't deal, and you're his emotional support human.

Now I am forced to talk. If nothing else, to explain why I don't want to talk. Still true: I don't want to talk about you, or to hear others talk about you.

I want to quote Wittgenstein on the unspeakable and the necessity for silence. Even if quoting philosophers out of context was something you told us not to do. Philosophical statements aren't *old sayings*, you said.

A pause here to wonder at Wittgenstein, three of whose four brothers killed themselves, and who often thought about killing himself too. Who, like Kafka, is said to have received the news of his terminal illness with relief, but whose words at the actual hour of death bring to mind George Bailey: Tell them I've had a wonderful life!

Do I talk to Apollo, the shrink asks. Well, yes. To encourage bonding, it is recommended that people talk to their dogs. Which seems to come naturally (though my guess is people are now doing it less and less, thanks to our attention-devouring devices).

I once heard a stranger in agitated conversation with her pug: And I suppose it's all *my* fault again, isn't it? At which, I swear, the dog rolled its eyes.

Yes, I talk to Apollo. But not about you. That's the thing: I don't have to tell *him*. (*Dogs are the best mourners in the world, as everyone knows.* Joy Williams.)

And just because there are other people who've lost someone to suicide doesn't mean that what I'm feeling is something that can be shared. I did once sit through a radio program on the subject of suicide loss. Listeners were invited to call in and comment. All the usual word-stones were cast: sinful, spiteful, cowardly, vengeful, irresponsible. Sick. No one doubted that the suicide had been in the wrong. A right to commit suicide simply did not exist. Monsters of selfishness and self-pity, suicides were. Such ingratitude for the precious gift of life. And although they might hate themselves, it was not themselves suicides wished to destroy so much as the family and friends they left behind.

None of this was helpful.

But neither were the dozen or so books on suicide that I read this past year. I did learn some interesting things. For example, that certain ancient sages held that voluntary death, though generally to be condemned, could be morally acceptable, even honorable, as an escape from unbearable pain, melancholy, or disgrace—or even just plain old boredom. That later thinkers have suggested that, despite Christianity's absolute prohibition against committing suicide (though nowhere in the entire Bible is there any explicit condemnation of it), Christ himself could be said to have done just that. That in Western countries the volume of suicide notes reached a peak during the eighteenth century, when they were usually intended to appear, alongside other public announcements, in the newspapers.

And this kicker: Writing in the first person is a known sign of suicide risk.

What was helpful: words of a woman I knew years ago, when we happened to be working at the same magazine. Out of the blue, when they were young and newly wed, her husband had made her a widow. One day we were planning our future, she said, the next day he was gone. At first I thought I owed it to him to do everything possible to try to understand. But I came to believe this was wrong. He had chosen silence. His death was a mystery. In the end I decided I should leave him his silence. His mystery.

I talk about my feeling of living with one foot in madness, the distortions of reality, the fog that descends at certain moments, unsettling as amnesia. (What am I doing in this classroom? Why, in *this* mirror, does my face look so weird? *I* wrote that? What could I have meant?)

I talk about how, no matter how much I sleep, I'm exhausted. About the number of times I bump into something, or drop something, or trip over my own feet. Stepping off the curb into the path of a car that would have struck me if someone standing by hadn't jerked me back. The days when I don't eat, the days when I eat nothing but junk. Absurd fears: What if there's a gas leak and the building blows up? Losing or misplacing stuff. Forgetting to do my taxes.

These are all symptoms of bereavement, the therapist tells me unnecessarily. Doctor Obvious.

But you know, Apollo, I say after my fourth or fifth session, I think I really am beginning to feel a little better.

Another thing about Wittgenstein. According to the physicist Freeman Dyson, who attended Wittgenstein's lectures at Cambridge in 1946, if a woman dared to appear in the lecture room he would remain silent until she got the message and left.

I get stupider and stupider every day, Dyson once overheard the philosopher mutter repeatedly under his breath.

About women, at any rate.

Tempted to put too much faith in the great male mind, remember this: It looked at cats and declared them gods. It looked at women and asked, Are they human? And, once that hard nut had been cracked: But do they have souls?

It's not that I can't say how I feel. It's very simple. I miss you. I miss you every day. I miss you very much.

Another pause, this time to wonder what *Wittgenstein* meant by "a wonderful life"?

And to feel for his sister Gretl: three brothers *and* a husband who suicided.

I tell the therapist about those uncanny moments, after I first heard the news, when I believed there'd been a mistake. You were gone but not dead. More like you were just missing. Like you'd decided to play some horrid juvenile trick on us. You were missing, not dead. Meaning you could come back. You could come back, and if you could come back, of course you would. Akin to that brief period years ago when I believed it was just stress or fatigue or some odd phase I was going through, and once whatever the trouble was had passed my looks would come back.

Later I found myself often recalling a scene, the final scene, from the movie *Houdini*. I'm talking about the old fifties version, with Tony Curtis, which I saw on TV when I was a teen. He who had become world famous for his spectacular escapes dies while attempting to break out of the water tank in which he's been submerged upside down with his feet locked in stocks. The Chinese Water Torture Cell trick he'd pulled off before, but this time, unknown to spectators, he is weak and in pain from a ruptured appendix.

Dying, the master magician promises his wife: If there's any way, I'll come back.

Which gave me goose bumps then and still has the power to move me.

Even if I know that the real Houdini died in a hospital bed, and that his last words were *I'm tired of fighting*.

I drag up another memory. This time I'm much younger: a child. Birthday party at the house of a friend, a large slate-gray Victorian, to me a creepy castle. Hide-and-seek. I am It. I finish counting and uncover my eyes. It is late afternoon, it is winter, and all the lights have been turned off for the game. Filled just minutes ago with bright boisterous life, the house is now a tomb.

I was told that the first ones to leave their hiding places to investigate found me sprawled facedown on the carpet.

Too much excitement, too much ice cream and cake: the grown-ups got it wrong, the way grown-ups will get children's troubles wrong. And I, frightened to the core, and not having the words, didn't even try to enlighten them. But I never forgot. The tired phrase *deathly still* can bring it all back in a flash.

The year before, my grandfather had vanished. Followed shortly by our elementary school principal. Nothing that was said to explain these vanishing acts was very convincing. But that there was something nasty involved, some unspeakable thing about which lips must stay sealed—this was clear.

The horror sank in. They weren't hiding, the other kids; they were gone. Vanished into that same darkness, never to return. Only I—*It*—remained. Alone alone alone. The room swam before my eyes. I threw up before I fainted.

. . .

Remembering just now that Gretl Wittgenstein's father-in-law also took his own life.

Do I dream about you?

Dutifully I describe it: Wading through deep snow, struggling to catch up with someone far ahead, a figure in a dark coat, like a triangular tear in the vast white blanket. I call your name. You spin around, start semaphoring with your arms. But I don't understand. Are you telling me to hurry up, or warning me to stop and turn back? Agony of uncertainty. End of dream. Or, I say (for some absurd reason apologetically), at least that's all I remember.

I talk about the times I see you. Each time my heart turns over. But why should it be that almost always the person I mistake for you is someone who looks like you not at the age when you died but at some other stage of your life. Once, on campus, I nearly shout for joy at the sight of someone who looks like you when you and I first met.

I confess to sudden rages. Walking in Midtown, rush hour's peak, people streaming in both directions, I find myself seething, ready to kill. Who are all these fucking people, and how is it fair, how is it even possible that all of them, these perfectly ordinary people, should be alive, when *you*—

The therapist interrupts to point out that you made a choice.

It's true that I keep forgetting this. Because very often it seems to me that it's not what happened, that it wasn't a choice at all, no act of free will, but rather some freak accident that befell you.

Which, I suppose, is not inaccurate, self-homicide being unquestionably against the natural order of things.

Why should a dog, a horse, a rat have life and thou no breath at all? weeps King Lear. *Thou* being his daughter Cordelia.

At times I can barely contain my anger at students. How can you be an English major and not know that you don't put a period after a question mark? Why do even graduate students not know the difference between a novel and a memoir, and why do they keep referring to full-length books as "pieces"?

I want to hit the student whose excuse for not doing that week's assigned reading of fifty pages is that she had jury duty.

I delete without answering the questionnaire from someone who is considering taking my class. (Number one: *Are you overconcerned with things like punctuation and grammar?*)

All that anger, says the therapist. Yet none directed at *you*. No anger, no blame. Is this because I think suicide can be justifiable?

Plato thought so. Seneca thought so.

But what do *I* think? Why do I think you did it?

Because you were trapped upside down in a tankful of water.

Because you were weak and in pain.

Because you were tired of fighting.

. . .

Once, I spend most of the hour not saying anything. Each time I start to speak I break down. After a few tries, I give up and sit there sobbing until it's time to go.

I wanted to talk about the time you and I met up in Berlin. I'd been living there that year, on a fellowship. You were passing through: the German translation of your latest book had just been published. So we had a long weekend together.

You wanted to visit the grave site of the writer Heinrich von Kleist, the very place where, in 1811, at the age of thirty-four, he shot himself. I knew the story. How Kleist, who suffered all his life from despair, had for a long time wanted to die. But not alone. The idea of a suicide pact had always turned him on. His dream lover: a woman whose heart's desire would be to die with him.

Henriette Vogel was not the first woman he approached, but it was she who, diagnosed with terminal cancer at the age of thirty-one, rapturously accepted his proposal of a romantic murder-suicide.

After shooting her in the left breast, Kleist shot himself in the mouth. The man's job.

Both appear to have expected the experience to be an orgasmic one.

A witness reported having seen them the night before, relaxed and dining in merry spirits. And although the two were

Christians, they appear also to have expected that death would transport them to a better world, an eternity of bliss among angels—no fears of the eternal torture said to await equally the violent against others and the violent against themselves.

Vogel, who was married, asked in a last letter to her husband not to be separated from Kleist in death. They were buried where they fell, a shady green slope on the lake known as the Kleiner Wannsee.

Like many burial grounds, this one was peaceful. I would return to it often by myself. (The site has since been renovated, but I've never been back.) Almost always I found a fresh flower resting on Kleist's tombstone, even in winter. I had loved his work ever since reading it for the first time in college, and it pleased me to be at his resting place. To think of the Brothers Grimm walking there. Rilke on the very spot, writing verses in his notebook.

Crossing the Wannsee bridge that day, we saw two swans mating. Not the graceful sight one might have thought—the female looked in serious danger of being drowned. In any case, it was hard to imagine their comical flapping efforts succeeding.

But not long after, on a walkway under the bridge, I found their nest, surprisingly close to shore. Here, too, I would often return. Usually, I'd find one—the female, I assumed—either curled sleeping or sitting on the nest, while the other floated nearby. Sometimes I watched them working together, enlarging the nest with twigs and rushes until it resembled a giant Mexican hat.

It is common knowledge that swans mate for life. A less well-known fact is that they sometimes cheat. I myself discovered that one of this pair—the male, I assumed—habitually visited another swan, in a different part of the lake.

Though I never saw any eggs in the nest, I was hoping in due time to see some cygnets. But then one day the nest was gone. I have no idea what happened to it. The swans began building a new nest, but before long it too vanished.

The swans in Wannsee often appeared toward the end of the day, their feathers taking on the changing colors of the sunset. Rose-tinted swans, swans as pink as flamingos, as blue as violets, swans the deep purple of twilight, night swans. Birds out of a dream, a reminder of the beauty of the world. Of heaven.

He must have been a monster, we agreed. Using his poetic powers to talk a meek, incurably sick woman into letting herself be shot.

But what about her? She was dying anyway. Suicide by proxy, while hastening her death, almost certainly spared her much suffering. But enabling another person to commit murder and self-murder—in this case someone who, though in despair, was still young, and who might have lived and continued to create literature of genius for many more years—how justify that?

If Kleist had never found a death buddy—if, like others before her, this woman had refused his mad request—who knows what might have happened? Or not happened. In fact, the more I think about it, the more it seems to me that Madame Vogel has a lot to answer for. What kind of love was this? Did it not even occur to her to try and save him?

Now wondering why I wrote "Of heaven" when I don't believe such a place exists.

For those who don't want to go it alone, the internet is a godsend. Perfect strangers, sometimes living far apart, find each other online and arrange a date. A man from Norway flies to New Zealand where he and another man jump from a cliff. A man and a woman book separate rooms at a lakeside resort and are later found handcuffed and drowned together. In Japan, where the trend for group suicide is especially strong, carloads of corpses keep turning up. But the favorite suicide site in Japan remains the famous Aokigahara Forest, at the foot of Mount Fuji, where neither trail signs saying things like *You are not alone* and *Think of your parents* nor phones connected to hotlines have succeeded in ousting it from its place as one of the top suicide destinations in the world. Vying with the Golden Gate Bridge, number one spot in the US.

Berlin. I remember you were in excellent spirits. In one of those flukes of publishing (which, according to you, was now mostly flukes), your book, which had sold poorly back home, was a bestseller in Europe. So you were given the royal treatment on that tour. You were delighted to be in Germany, known for its serious readers (as you kept saying), and particularly in Berlin, one of your favorite cities, like Paris an ideal walking city, rich in the tradition of flânerie.

I remember how happy I was when I heard you were coming. I'd been missing you a lot. And, partly because this was one of those rare times when you were single, and partly because we were far from home—visitors abroad who were often assumed, naturally enough, to be husband and wife—it sometimes felt as if that's what we were: a couple. A couple on vacation. At any rate, I remember feeling especially close to you that weekend and sadly bereft when you left.

All of this is branded in memory and was much on my mind as I sat in the therapist's office. But I could not talk about it because I could not stop crying.

Now asking myself why, in spite of reflection, I let "Of heaven" stand.

He thinks I'm in love with you. He thinks I've always been in love with you. This he tells me in a voice that's different from his usual gentle one, not exactly ungentle but a touch impatient if I'm not mistaken. Or maybe just urgent.

This complicates the bereavement process, he explains. I am mourning you as a lover would. As a wife would.

Maybe it will help you to write about it, he says the last time I see him.

And maybe it won't.

I had forgotten how painful it is to remember, writes one of my students. And she is only eighteen years old.

It is Hector who brings the news, ringing my bell one late afternoon. The building management agent has advised the landlord that it's not worth the trouble of contesting my request to keep Apollo as a support animal, especially since there have been no complaints about him from other tenants. (A friend points out that now that I have the certificate I could probably get away with having a dog in my apartment as long as I live there, even after Apollo has passed. Probably, but I have promised myself not to pull this trick more than once. And besides, I can't bear to think of Apollo *passed*, Apollo *replaced*.)

Hector is grinning from ear to ear. I am damp-eyed with relief.

I think this calls for a celebration, I say.

And as it happens I still have that bottle of champagne my student gave me.

PART TEN

Anyone forced to contemplate an aging pet is like the poet Gavin Ewart wishing that his fourteen-year-old convalescent cat might get to have just one more summer before *that last fated hateful journey to the vet.*

I see the gray hairs on Apollo's muzzle and the redness rimming his eyes, I see how stiffly he walks some days, how it sometimes takes two efforts for him to get to his feet, and I ache. The list of things the vet gives me to watch out for, common signs of disease and deterioration in senior dogs, makes me quail. (*How are you going to take care of him if he becomes infirm?*) In the six months between checkups, his arthritis has gotten worse.

One miracle is not enough. That disaster has been averted, that we are spared separation or eviction—I'm sorry, but it's not enough. Now I am like the Fisherman's Wife: I want more. And not just another summer, or two or three or four. I want Apollo to live as long as I do. Anything less is unfair.

And why, in the end, that *inevitable* trip to the vet? Why can't he die at home, in his sleep, peacefully, like a good dog deserves?

Why, having saved him, must I now watch him suffer—suffer and die—and then be left alone, without him?

I think he knows when I'm having such thoughts. If he's nearby, he will turn his attention to me, almost as if to distract me.

It is widely believed that although animals don't know that one day they'll die, many of them do know when they're actually dying. So at what point does a dying animal become aware of what's happening? Could it possibly be a long time before? And how do animals respond to aging? Are they completely puzzled, or do they somehow intuit what the signs mean? Are these foolish questions? I acknowledge that they are. And yet they preoccupy me.

Apollo has a favorite toy, a bright red tug toy made of hard rubber. I like the mock monster-dog noises he makes when we play tug-of-war. But most of the fun for him seems to be in letting me win. (I remain ignorant as to how aware he is or is not of his own strength; I've certainly never seen him use anything like the full force of it.) Other toys don't interest him, though I keep buying new ones—as I keep taking him to the dog park, even though I've lost hope of seeing him play there. He is no more interested in other dogs than he is in other people. And this continues to bother me. *Why won't you play? So many nice friendly dogs at the park!*

But why should this matter? I guess it's like a parent wanting their kid to be, if not wildly popular, at least not a loner. I'd be so happy to see him make friends with just one other dog, maybe even fall in love. Just because he's been neutered doesn't mean he can't have special feelings for another dog, does it? We often run into a stunning silver Italian mastiff named Bella. (Anthropomorphism, I've decided, is inescapable, and though I might try to hide it I no longer fight it.)

On the much admired trait of canine loyalty, the writer Karl Kraus has pointed out that it's to people that dogs are loyal, not to other dogs. And so: maybe not the best example of the virtue. In fact, very often, dogs hate other dogs, even their own blood.

I saw it again just this morning. Two leashed dogs catch sight of each other and instantly start lunging and snarling.

Motherfucker. I hate you. Goddamn you. I'll bite your fucking nose off, you stinking piece of shit. I'll kill you. Lucky for you I'm on this leash, or I'd tear your fucking balls off.

All but choking themselves to death as they strain to get at each other.

Apollo is not like that. I have never seen him insult or attack or bully another dog. In spite of all he's been through, he has remained kind, he has kept his—humanity, I want to say (what word *should* I say?).

One time we pass a stoop with a cat sitting at about the same level as Apollo's head. The cat jumps up, goes horseshoe, and spits in his face. Apollo turns the other cheek: a paw shoots out and swipes it. For an instant I fear for the cat, but Apollo keeps walking. He doesn't want trouble. He wants peace.

Even in old age, he is a creature of such arresting beauty that he regularly draws gasps.

To think what he was like in his prime.

It's not uncommon to wish to have known what a person you've come to love was like before you met them. It hurts, almost, not to have known what a beloved was like as a child. I have felt this way about every man I've ever been in love with, and about many close friends as well, and now it's how I feel about Apollo.

Not to have known him as a frisky young dog, to have missed his entire puppyhood! I don't feel just sad, I feel cheated. Not even a photo to show what he was like. I have to make do with looking at harlequin Great Dane puppies in books, or online. An activity to which I confess I have devoted some hours.

It's happened just once. Walking in SoHo, I run into another person walking a harlequin Dane. Both humans are thrilled, but the dogs look right past each other.

.   .   .

Something bad happens to the dog: a lesson learned early, from childhood books. The animals in those stories often die, often in bad ways. Old Yeller. The red pony. And even when they don't die, even when they're not just alive but happy at the end, they suffer, often badly, often they are put through hell. Black Beauty. Flicka. White Fang. Buck. The autobiography of Beautiful Joe, based on the life of a real dog and abounding in scenes of cruelty, begins with his brute owner slicing off Joe's ears and tail with an ax.

No doubt like many other readers, I remember crying over these books (never so hard as over poor Joe), yet never regretting having read them. Is there anything more compelling than a story about a child and an animal who bond? When I first knew I wanted to write, I was sure this was what I would write about. But I never did.

When people are very young they see animals as equals, even as kin. That humans are different, unique and superior to all other species—this they have to be taught.

Children fantasize about a world populated solely by non-humans. I liked to pretend that I was some kind of animal, a cat or a rabbit or a horse. I would try to communicate through animal sounds rather than speech and refused to eat with my hands. At times I kept this up for so long and with such conviction that it became cause for parental concern. A game, but at the core of it something dead serious, a trace of which has been carried into adulthood: the wish not to be part of the human race.

Something bad happens to the dog in Milan Kundera's novel *The Unbearable Lightness of Being.* The dog is given as a pup by the main protagonist, Tomas, to his wife, Tereza—for the very same reason, we are told, that he married Tereza: to make up for the pain and humiliation his incorrigible womanizing causes her. Though female, the pup is whimsically named after a male character in another novel: Anna Karenina's husband. Karenin the dog hates change, loves being in the country, where he makes friends with a pig, and, after developing terminal cancer, is put to sleep.

Kundera has his own interpretation of Genesis 1:26. *True human goodness can come to the fore only when its recipient has no power.* Let it be seen, then, how the human race treats those that have been placed at its mercy. And put to this moral test, *mankind has suffered . . . a debacle so fundamental that all others stem from it.*

Karenin and Tereza are devoted to each other. Reflecting on their pure and selfless bond, Tereza concludes that such love is, if not bigger, nevertheless better than the corrupt, fraught, eternally disappointing and compromised thing she has always had with Tomas.

Idyllic is how Kundera describes human relationships with

animals. Idyllic because animals were not expelled with us from Paradise. There they remain, untroubled by such complications as the separation of body and soul, and it's through our love and friendship with them that we are able to reconnect to Paradise, albeit by just a thread.

Others go further. Dogs are not merely untouched by evil. They are celestial beings, angels incarnate, furry guardian spirits sent to watch over and help people live. Like the deification of cats, this belief is all over the internet, and growing. It makes you wonder. About people, I mean.

Something very bad happens to a lot of dogs in *Disgrace*. The question persists, why won't David Lurie save the one, a mutt that has clearly come to love him and for which he, in turn, feels a special affection. Why can't that dog—a good dog, crippled but still young, and apparently sensitive to music—be spared the fate of all the other unwanted dogs destroyed at the animal welfare clinic? Why, instead of keeping this one dog, does Lurie insist on sacrificing it?

Remember Agent Starling in *The Silence of the Lambs* telling Hannibal Lecter how, as a little girl living on her uncle's ranch, she had desperately wanted to save the lambs from the spring slaughter. How she picked up one lamb and tried to run away. *I thought if I could save just one . . . but he was heavy. So heavy.* In the end, like Lurie, she could not save an animal marked for death. Not even one.

We know they think, but do dogs have opinions?

Kundera makes much of the fact that, unlike us, animals don't feel disgust. I'm not so sure about this (not even cats?), but that dogs are not critical or judgmental is undeniably a big part of what endears them to us. (This is what made educators think having kids with reading problems read aloud to dogs was such a great idea. Also, perhaps, why performers like Laurie Anderson and Yo-Yo Ma have reported looking out at their concert audience and fantasizing that it's all dogs.)

Gratitude: I don't believe people are imagining it when they attribute this feeling to their rescue dog. I often feel that Apollo is grateful toward me.

I want to know if he looks forward to things. *She'll be home soon. Can't wait to eat! Tomorrow is another day.*

Even more, I want to know how he remembers the past. Does he have yearnings? Regrets? Sweet, sweet memories? Bittersweet ones? With senses as keen as theirs, why couldn't dogs have Proustian moments?

Why couldn't they have eureka moments, epiphanies, and so on?

In the beginning I sometimes caught him staring at me only to turn away when I looked back. Now he often rests his block of a head on my knees and tips his eyes at me with a speaking expression.

What do you talk to him about? the shrink wanted to know.

Mostly I seem to ask questions. What's up, pup? Did you have a nice nap? Were you chasing something in your sleep? Do you want to go out? Are you hungry? Are you happy? Does your arthritis hurt? Why won't you play with other dogs? *Are* you an angel? Do you want me to read to you? Do you want me to sing? Who loves you? Do you love me? Will you love me forever? Do you wanna dance? Am I the best person you've ever had? Can you tell I've been drinking? Do these jeans make me look fat?

If we could talk to the animals, goes the song.

Meaning, if they could talk to us.

But of course that would ruin everything.

Your whole house smells of dog, says someone who comes to visit. I say I'll take care of it. Which I do by never inviting that person to visit again.

One night I wake to find Apollo by the bed, apparently trying with his teeth to draw back over me the blanket I must have thrown off in my sleep. When I tell people about this they don't believe it. They say I must have dreamed it. Which I agree is possible. But really I'm thinking they're just jealous.

At a book party. A woman I've never met before giggles and says, Aren't you the one who's in love with a dog?

Am I? Have I taken a dog husband as Ackerley took a dog

wife? Will his death be the saddest day of my life? Will I too want to immolate myself as a suttee? No. But I too have found myself so eager to get home to him that I have jumped in a cab rather than take the train. I too sing with joy at the thought of seeing him, and for sure, this love is not like any love I've ever felt before.

A recurring anxiety: Someone claiming to be Apollo's owner finally shows up, someone with a crazy but convincing tale of how the two of them got separated, and now I'm expected to give him up.

Reminded here that I only recently learned that the term *puppy love* refers to the feeling a person might have *for* a puppy. Nothing to do, as I'd thought, with a puppy's feelings for a person.

Reading Ackerley, I noticed that he sometimes uses the word *person* when referring to a dog. At first I thought this was a mistake. But, considering that he was one of the most careful writers in the world, I'd say this is unlikely.

Now reminded of a friend of mine who told me that, for years, he thought the expression was *It's a doggy-dog world* and was never quite sure what it meant.

When they see you with a dog, people tell you dog stories. A man in a business suit strokes Apollo's head as he tells me how his mother decided one day to abandon a dog she'd had for years. She brought the dog to a bus station and left it in its carrier under a bench. When the man found out, he tracked the dog down to a shelter. He called the shelter to say he'd take the dog, but at the moment he was across the country finishing up law school. The shelter promised to hold the dog, but before he could get there the dog died. He was told that it had simply stopped eating.

I just don't get it, the man tells me. The dog had been grossly fat because his mother used to feed him doughnuts, he says, but he was also still young and cute and totally adoptable. No way she needed to dump him like that. Though it had happened years ago, he was still trying to understand why his mother would've done such a thing.

Because she wanted to hurt someone, I don't say.

A public radio producer invites me to contribute a piece about a book, which can be any book I feel strongly about and would recommend to listeners, she says.

In fact, I am familiar with this series, having heard other writers reading on the air their pieces about their favorite books.

I choose *The Oxford Book of Death*. Not only because it's a book I really do think everyone should read, but also because I happen to be rereading it, with particular attention to the chapters "Suicide" and "Animals."

I write the requested five hundred words, praising the anthology's selection of extracts from ancient to present times on every aspect of the subject, from "Definitions" to "Last Words." I say how fascinating I found all this writing about death to be, how paradoxically entertaining and full of life the whole book was.

I spend a lot of time on the piece, grateful for the little assignment, to be writing something, anything. I finish it and send it off, but there is no response, and I never hear from the producer again.

In the news:

An experimental therapy being practiced at some animal shelters: having volunteers read aloud to abused and traumatized dogs.

Interview with a professional dancer who, as a young boy, a victim of persistent bullying, went mute.

Death of author Michael Herr. Whose obituary reveals that in the last years of his life he had become a devout Buddhist, and stopped writing.

From *The Oxford Book of Death*:

Nabokov's syllogism. *Other men die; but I am not another; therefore I'll not die.*

"The one experience I shall never describe," I said to Vita yesterday, journaled Virginia Woolf. Fifteen years before the undescribable took place.

. . .

In writing workshops, many stories begin with someone getting up in the morning. Much less often does a story end with someone going to bed. More likely a story will end with a death. In fact, many student stories either begin or end at a funeral. And when a student wants to convey a character's stream of thoughts, they almost always set the character in motion. They put him or her into some kind of transportation, usually a car or a plane. As if they could only imagine someone thinking if that person is also moving through space.

Q. Why did you send this character on a trip to India when that has nothing to do with the rest of the story?

A. I wanted to show him worrying a lot.

Last words. *So this is how the story ends*, my friend in the AIDS hospice said. Eyes wide with wonder, like a child's.

PART ELEVEN

How should the story end? For some time now I have imagined it ending like this.

A woman alone in her apartment one morning, getting ready to go out. One of those early spring days with equal periods of sun and clouds. Chance of a shower, late. The woman has been awake since first light.

What time is it now?

Eight o'clock.

What did the woman do between the time she woke up and eight?

For about half an hour she lay in bed trying to fall back to sleep.

Does the woman suffer from that particular kind of insomnia: frequent waking, inability to stay asleep?

Yes.

Is there some little trick she tries when this happens to get back to sleep?

Counting backward from a thousand. Naming, in alphabetical order, all the states. This morning, though, neither worked.

So she got up. And then—?

Made coffee. One espresso brewed in a single-cup moka pot that she acquired only recently and that she has found she likes better than the French press she'd been using before and that about a month ago she accidentally broke. In general, she enjoys this morning ritual. Brewing and drinking the coffee while listening to the news on the radio.

What news did the woman hear?

In fact, this morning she is preoccupied and hasn't really been listening.

Did she eat anything?

Half a banana sliced into a cup of plain yogurt mixed with some raisins and walnuts.

What did she do after breakfast?

Checked email. Responded to one message, an inquiry from the college bookstore about some books she'd ordered for a course. Confirmed a dentist appointment. Took a shower and began to get dressed. But she keeps wavering because of the kind of day it is. Will a sweater be too warm? Will her raincoat be too light? Should she take an umbrella? What about a hat? Gloves?

Where is the woman off to this morning?

To visit an old friend who's been in the hospital.

What does she finally decide to wear?

Jeans and a cardigan over a turtleneck. Her hooded raincoat.

How does the woman get to her friend's house?

She takes the subway from Manhattan to Brooklyn.

Does she stop anywhere on the way?

At a florist near the train station in Manhattan, where she buys some daffodils.

And when she gets off at her stop, does she go straight to her friend's house?

Yes. See her now approaching his brownstone.

Does the friend she is visiting also live alone?

No, he lives with his wife. Who isn't home this morning because she's at work. But there's a dog. Hear him bark at the sound of the doorbell. The door opens and the man steps out, greeting the woman with a hug. The man is dressed—by coincidence—just as she is under her raincoat: blue jeans, black turtleneck, gray cardigan. They hold each other tightly for a few moments as the dog, a miniature dachshund, barks and leaps at them.

Now they are settled in the living room, drinking the tea the man has made for them. A small plate holding a few shortbread cookies remains untouched. The daffodils have been placed in a small crystal vase in a sunny spot on the windowsill where they glow with a neon brightness that (the woman can't help thinking) makes them look fake. One of the stems has bent, and the flower hangs down as if ashamed, or shy of the spotlight.

Now it can be seen that the man has the paleness and gauntness of a convalescent. His voice is strained, as if it's an effort to speak above a whisper. There is stress in the air as of something about to burst or break. The dog senses this and for that reason is unable to relax, though he lies very still in his wicker basket. The man speaks, and the dog, hearing his name, beats his tail.

"I wanted to thank you again for taking care of Jip."

"Oh, he was no trouble," says the woman. "I liked having him. It was like having a furry bit of you there."

"Ha," goes the man, and the woman says, "I was just glad to be able to help."

"And you were a *big* help," the man assures her. "Jip's a good boy, but he's spoiled and needs a lot of attention. And my poor wife had enough to deal with." A pause. The man lowers his voice. "By the way, I meant to ask, what exactly did she tell you?"

"That she was on a business trip and her flight was delayed because of a storm in Denver. That she tried calling you from the airport but there was no answer. Then the flight was canceled and she took a cab home, and when she got there she saw the note to the cleaning lady warning her not to come in. And to call 911."

The man does not look at the woman as she speaks. He stares at the daffodils on the windowsill, squinting as if their brightness hurts his eyes. When she stops speaking he waits, as if expecting more, and when there is no more he says, "If a student put that in a story I'd say, That's too easy."

At that moment a cloud blots the sun and the room darkens. The woman has a surge of panic, alarmed at the stinging threat of tears.

"I had it all worked out," the man says. "I'd taken Jip to the kennel. The cleaning lady was scheduled to come the next morning."

"But how are you now?" asks the woman a bit too loudly, making the dog startle. "How do you feel?"

"Disgraced."

The woman starts to protest but the man cuts her off. "It's true. I feel humiliated. But that's a common response."

I know, the woman doesn't say. I've been reading up on suicide.

"But that's not all I feel," the man says, lifting his chin. "Turns out I'm nothing special. I'm like most failed suicides: happy to have survived."

At a loss the woman says, "Well, that's good to hear!"

"I keep wondering, though, why I don't feel *more*," the man goes on. "A lot of the time I feel hazy, or numb, like it all happened fifty years ago—or never even at all. But that's partly the medication."

The cloud has moved on and the light pours in again.

"You must be glad to be home," says the woman.

The man pauses. "I'm certainly glad to be out of the hospital. It felt more like months than a couple of weeks. There really isn't a whole lot to do on a psych ward. What made it even worse was that I couldn't read, my concentration was shot, I'd forget each sentence as soon as I got to the end of it. And because I didn't want people to know what happened, I couldn't exactly have visitors. By the way, you're still the only one outside the family who knows the whole story. For now I want to keep it that way."

The woman nods.

"Not that it was a totally negative experience," he adds. "And I kept reminding myself: When something bad happens to a writer, no matter how terrible, there's always a silver lining."

"Oh?" says the woman, sitting up straight. "Does that mean you're going to write about it?"

"That's certainly possible."

"As fiction, or memoir?"

"I have no idea. It's too soon. I'd need to get some distance from it."

"And are you writing now? Have you been able to write?"

"Well, in fact, that was something I wanted to tell you about. We had a little workshop on the ward! Part of group therapy. There was this woman, a recreational therapist as they're called. She had us write poetry instead of prose—because we didn't have lots of time, she said, but no doubt also for other reasons. And she had everyone read what they wrote out loud. No analysis, no criticism. Just sharing, you know. Everyone wrote the most appalling stuff and everyone else gushed over it. All this dreadful poetry that *wasn't* poetry—you can imagine the sort of thing. Voices trembling and cracking, some taking forever to get through it. And everyone was completely in earnest, you could tell how much it meant to them to have a chance to spill their guts and see that they could move people to tears. And oh, were there ever tears. And every poem got a round of applause. It was very strange. In all my years of teaching I've never come close to the kind of emotion I felt in that room. It was very moving, very strange."

"It's hard for me even to imagine you in that situation."

"Believe me, the irony was not lost on me. At first I thought I didn't want any part of it, just like I didn't want any part of the coloring books they kept encouraging us to use—not just to pass the time but because coloring is supposed to reduce anxiety. But that was problematic because they all knew I was a writer and a writing teacher and I would've looked like the most awful snob. And as I say, life on the ward was so boring. I couldn't read, and I refused to go on any outings—I was terrified of running into some person I knew and having to explain what I was doing at the movies or a museum with a nurse and a gaggle of nutcases. If nothing else, the workshop was a distraction, a way to kill some time. And then, to be completely honest, there was the therapist. She wasn't gorgeous but she was young and she was kind of hot, and you know me. I wanted her attention. I might have been a mental patient, and old enough to be her gramps, but still I wanted to impress her. Really, I wanted to fuck her—not that there was any hope of that. Anyway, I hadn't written poetry since I was in college, and there was something quite wonderful about turning back to it after all those years. I'll remember that round of applause till I die. And the big surprise is, I've kept it up."

"You're writing poetry?" The woman feels another surge of panic as she thinks maybe she'll be asked to read some of this poetry. Or, worse, sit and listen to him read it to her.

"Oh, nothing that I'd show anyone at this point," the man says. "But right now it's easier for me to be working on short things. The idea of writing anything longer frankly scares the hell out of me. Going back to the book I was working on—like a dog to its vomit! But enough about me. What have you been up to?"

She tells the man about a new course she's teaching. Life and Story. Fiction as autobiography, autobiography as fiction. Writers like Proust, Isherwood, Duras, Knausgaard.

"Good luck getting the little fuckers to read Proust! And what about the piece you were working on? Did you finish?"

"No, I dropped it."

"Oh no! Why?"

The woman shrugs. "It didn't work out. Partly because I kept feeling guilty, like I was using the people I was writing about. I can't explain exactly why I felt that way, but I did. And you know how it is with guilt, it's like smoke and fire: you don't feel it for nothing."

"But that's nonsense," says the man. "Everything is material for the writer, it just depends on *how* you use it. Would I have encouraged you to write something I thought was wrong?"

"No. But the truth is that when you suggested that I write about those women you weren't thinking about them but about me. It was something that would be good for me. I would get published, I would get read, I would get paid."

"Yes, that's what writers do, it's called journalism. But you can't tell me there weren't other good reasons."

"Maybe, but it doesn't matter. Because the truth is, I couldn't do it. I mean literally. I would write something like 'Oksana is a twenty-two-year-old woman with a pale round face, high cheek-bones, and blond-streaked hair who speaks with a light Russian accent.' Then I would read what I wrote and feel nauseated. And I could not go on. The words would not come. I'd done all this research. I had all these notes. And I'd sit there and ask myself, what was I hoping to do with all this evidence of violence and cruelty, this catalog of atrocious details? Organize it into some engaging narrative? And if I did that, if I managed to find the precise words and the right tone—if I got the full true filthy horror of it down, in good clean prose—what would it mean? At the very least, I thought, writing should help *me*, the writer, un-derstand better, but I knew this was wishful thinking. Writing wasn't going to bring me any closer to understanding the kind of evil I was confronted with. And it wasn't going to do anything for the victims—that sad fact was also inescapable. The only thing I could say for sure, and which I believe is true in general for projects like this, was that the important person involved is always the writer. And I started to feel there was something not just selfish but cruel—cold-blooded, if you will—about what I was doing. I hated the forensic attitude that seems to be a requirement of the genre."

"Then maybe it would work better if you tried turning it into fiction," the man says.

The woman flinches. "Even worse. Making vivid, interesting characters out of those girls and women? Mythologizing and novelizing their suffering? *No.*"

The man gives an exaggerated sigh. "I know this argument, and I don't buy it. If everyone felt the way you do, the world would remain ignorant about things it has every good reason to know. Writers have to bear witness, it's their vocation. Some would say the writer *has* no higher calling than to bear witness to injustice and suffering."

"I've been thinking a lot about this since Svetlana Alexievich won the Nobel," says the woman. "The world is full of victims, says Alexievich. Ordinary people who experience horrific events but who are never heard and who end up forgotten. Her goal as a writer, she says, is to give these people words. But she doesn't believe it can be *done* through fiction. We're not living in the world of Chekhov anymore, she says, and fiction just isn't very good at getting at our reality. We need *documentary* fiction, stories cut from ordinary, individual life. No invention. No authorial point of view. She calls her books novels in voices. I've also heard them called evidence novels. Most of her narrators are women. She thinks women make better narrators because they examine their lives and feelings in ways men usually don't, more intensely and—why are you smiling?"

"I was just thinking about the argument that men should stop writing altogether."

"Alexievich doesn't say that. But she does argue that if you want to get at the depths of human experience and emotions you need to let women speak."

"But silence the writer herself."

"Right. The goal is to have those who actually live the suffering also do the witnessing, with the writer's role restricted to empowering them."

"It's become entrenched, hasn't it. This idea that what writers do is essentially shameful and that we're all somehow suspect characters. When I was teaching I noticed that, each year, my students' opinion of writers seemed to have sunk a little lower. But what does it mean when people who want to be writers see writers in such a negative light? Can you imagine a dance student feeling that way about the New York City Ballet? Or young athletes despising Olympic champions?"

"No. But dancers and athletes aren't seen as privileged, and writers are. To become a professional writer in our society you have to be privileged to begin with, and the feeling is that privileged people shouldn't be writing anymore—not unless they can find a way not to write about themselves, because that only furthers the agenda of white supremacy and the patriarchy. You scoff, but you can't deny that writing is an elitist, egotistic activity. You do it to get attention and to advance yourself in the world, you don't do it to make the world a more just place. Of course there's going to be some shame attached to it."

"I like what Martin Amis said: deploring egotism in novelists is like deploring violence in boxers. There was a time when everyone understood this. And there was a time when young writers believed that writing was a *vocation*—like being a nun or a priest, as Edna O'Brien said. Remember?"

"Yes, as I also remember Elizabeth Bishop saying there's nothing more embarrassing than being a poet. The problem of self-loathing isn't new. What's new is the idea that it's the people with the history of greatest injustice who have the greatest right to be heard, and that the time has come for the arts not just to make room for them but to be dominated by them."

"It's kind of a double bind, though, isn't it. The privileged shouldn't write about themselves, because that furthers the agenda of the imperialist white patriarchy. But they also shouldn't write about other groups, because that would be cultural appropriation."

"That's why I find Alexievich so interesting. If you're going to put an oppressed group to literary use, you need to find a way to let them speak and keep yourself out of it. The reason people now cringe at the idea that you have to be gifted in order to write is that it leaves too many voices out. Alexievich makes it possible for people to be heard, to get their stories told, whether they can write beautiful sentences or not. Another suggestion is that if you write about an oppressed group you should donate your fee to some cause that helps them."

"Which defeats the purpose if you need to make a living. In fact, under those rules, only the rich could afford to write whatever they wanted! Well, for me, the only serious question is whether Alexievich's brand of nonfiction fiction produces work that's as good as fiction fiction. I myself am inclined to agree with people like Doris Lessing, who thought imagination does the better job of getting at the truth. And I don't buy this idea that fiction is no longer up to portraying reality. I'd say the problem lies elsewhere. That was another thing I noticed about the students: how self-righteous they've become, how intolerant they are of any weakness or flaw in a writer's character. And I'm not talking about blatant racism or misogyny. I'm talking about any tiny sign of insensitivity or bias, any proof of psychological trouble, neurosis, narcissism, obsessiveness, bad habits—any eccentricity. If a writer didn't come across as the kind of person they'd want to have for a friend, which invariably meant someone progressive and clean-living, fuck 'em. I once had an entire class agree that it didn't matter how great a writer Nabokov was, a man like that—a snob and a pervert, as they saw him—shouldn't be on anyone's reading list. A novelist, like any good citizen, has to conform, and the idea that a person could write exactly what they wanted regardless of anyone else's opinion was unthinkable to them. Of course literature can't do its job in a culture like that. It upsets me how writing has become so politicized, but my students are more than okay with this. In fact, some of them want to be writers precisely *because* of this. And if you object to any of it, if you try talking to them about, say, art for art's sake, they cover their ears, they accuse you of profsplaining. That's why I've decided not to go back to teaching. Not to be too self-pitying, but when one is so at odds with the culture and its themes of the moment, what's the point."

And not to be too cruel, she doesn't say, but you will not be missed.

"Anyway, I'm sorry you gave up on that piece," he says. "You know I wanted you to finish it."

"To be honest," says the woman, "there was another reason. I got distracted. I started writing something else."

"What about?"

"About you."

"Me! How bizarre. What on earth made you decide to write about me?"

"Well, I didn't exactly plan it. It was around Christmas, and I happened to watch that movie *It's a Wonderful Life.* I'm sure you've seen it."

"Many times."

"And you know how it goes. Jimmy Stewart—George Bailey—is stopped from taking his own life by an angel who shows him what a great loss to the world it would've been had he never existed. I was sitting there watching with Jip—I had Jip in my lap—and of course I thought about you. I mean, I was always thinking about you after I heard what happened, wondering if you were going to be all right." (Here the man's gaze is again drawn to the flowers on the windowsill.) "I was thinking about what a close call it was. And I forgot all about the movie and started imagining what it would've been like if *you* hadn't been stopped. After all, it was sheer luck—or maybe *you* have a guardian angel. In any case, I could not stop thinking about it. What if you hadn't been found in time? And I knew that's what I needed to be writing about."

If the man was pale before, he is now as white as paper. "Am I hearing you right? Please say no."

"I'm sorry," the woman says. "I should have said that it's fiction. I disguised everyone."

"Oh, give me a break. You think I don't know what that means? *You changed my name.*"

"Actually, I didn't use names. I unnamed everyone. Except for the dog."

"Jip? Jip's in it, too?"

"Well, not exactly Jip. There's a dog. He's an important character. And he has a name: Apollo."

"Rather a grand name for a miniature dachshund, don't you think?"

"He's not a dachshund anymore. As I said, it's fiction, everything's different. Well, not everything. For example, I kept the detail about your finding him in the park. But you know how it works. You take some things from life, you make other things up, you tell a lot of half-lies and half-truths. So Jip becomes a Great Dane. And I made you an Englishman."

The man groans. "Couldn't you at least have made me Italian?"

The woman laughs. "Here's what I learned from Christopher Isherwood about turning a real person into a fictional character. It's like when you fall in love, he says. The fictional character is like the beloved: always extraordinary, never just another person. So you leave out the details about how that person is just like every other human being. Instead, you take what you find exciting or intriguing about them, the special things that made you want to write about them in the first place, and you exaggerate those. I know everyone wants to be Italian. But ever since I've known you you've always seemed like a Brit to me."

"And did you decide to make me a goy while you were at it?"

The woman laughs again. "No. But I did make you a bit more of a womanizer than you really are."

"Just a bit?"

"Ah. You're upset."

"You must have known I would be."

"I did. I admit that I did. When do people ever like it when you write about them? But I had to do something. As I said, from the minute I heard what had happened I could not stop thinking about it. So I did what you do if you're a writer and you're obsessed about something: you turn it into a story that you hope will lay it to rest, or at least help you figure out what it means. Even if we know from experience that this pretty much never actually works."

"Yes, I know, you don't have to tell me all this. *And writers really are like vampires*, you don't have to tell me that either, I'm sure it's something I once told you. Again, the irony is not lost on me. But as you can see you've given me quite a shock. I don't know what to think. What have you done? Right now I can tell you it feels like a betrayal. Absolutely a betrayal. And after the conversation we just had, I do have to ask: What makes *me* fair game? And you could at least have waited. Christ. There I am in the hospital, at the lowest moment of my entire life, and you're at the computer churning out pages. Not a very pretty picture. No. In fact, it strikes me as downright sleazy. What kind of friend— oh shame on you. Words fail you, I see. I'm amazed that you can even look me in the face. And did I hear you right, about a dog? The *dog* is a major character? Please say nothing bad happens to the dog."

DEFEAT THE BLANK PAGE!

PART TWELVE

This is the life, eh? Sunshine, not too hot, nice breeze, birdsong. Now, I know you like the sun, or you wouldn't be lying in it, you'd be up here on the shady porch with me. In fact, that sun must feel awfully good on your old bones. And you probably find the ocean breeze as refreshing as I do. Whenever it blows our way you lift your head to sniff, and I know your three hundred million odor receptors are picking up far more than the salty tang coming through my measly six million. It's hard for a person to smell more than one thing at a time. When I hear someone describe a wine as having a heavy black-pepper aroma followed by hints of raspberry and blackberry, I know they're full of shit. Show me the human that can smell a raspberry from a blackberry, even without having to go through pepper first. But *your* nose, on the other hand, tens of thousands of times as sensitive as mine, according to dog science—able to smell one rotten apple in two million barrels—now that's a whole other organ.

More amazing yet that you can tell apart the countless different scents hitting you at all times from every direction. A power like that makes *every* dog Wonder Dog. But talk about too much information. A power like that would drive any human being insane.

Thinking back to when you used to wake me in the middle of the night, inhaling every inch of me as I lay on the floor. Searching for data. Who was I and what might I have up my sleeve. You still sniff me all the time, but never with the same kind of investigative fervor.

According to science, you can smell not only what I had for breakfast today but also yesterday's dinner; when I last washed the shorts and T-shirt I'm wearing and whether or not I used bleach; where these sandals have taken me lately, and the fact that I've changed my brand of sunscreen. All of this would be a piece of cake for you. But now that I know what dogs can do, nothing would surprise me. The woman we often meet walking her mother and daughter mutts says dogs can tell time. When I come home from work, she says, I look up and see my girls at the window while I'm still a block away. They can tell from the level of my scent in the air.

I think it's fair to say that, thanks to your superior gift, you can read me better than I can read you. Hormones and phero-mones keep you updated. My anxiety about classes starting up again in a week. My open wounds. My hidden fears. My loneli-ness. My rage. My never-ending grief. You can smell all that.

What else. A fraction of malignant cells not yet detectable to medicine? Plaques and tangles silently forming in my brain, her-alds of dementia?

It's been surmised that a canine companion could know that its person is pregnant before that person herself knows.

Ditto a person dying.

Not that your sense of smell is what it used to be. Age has surely dulled it, as happens to people too. And look at that nose: once a ripe dripping black plum, now crusty and gray like a used coal.

I was saying: hot sun, cool breeze—these I'm pretty sure you like. But what about the birdsong. There's a feeder in the yard, and birds are abundant. We hear chickadees, sparrows, finches, and robins throughout the day—except for certain hours when, mysteriously, every one falls silent as if they'd all gone off to church.

I like bird sounds, even the monotonous woe-is-me of the mourning doves and the screechy cries of jays, crows, and gulls. But you, indifferent to man-made music of any sort, what effect does nature's music have on you?

I've known people who don't at all appreciate birdsong, who

even find it annoying. A story about the conductor Serge Koussevitzky complaining about being woken up mornings at Tanglewood by *all those birds singing out of tune.*

Sometimes a bird catches your eye—as pigeons in the city sometimes do—flying low through the air or hopping on the lawn, but never tempting you to the chase.

Squirrels, rabbits, and chipmunks also appear, some daring to get quite close, but none needing to fear.

The neighbor's tom, black and white like you, observes you through slitted eyes from the edge of the lawn, telegraphing that he's unimpressed.

Once, a strange-looking dog streaked by, furtive and swift, there and gone so fast that I might have hallucinated it. Only later did it hit me: that was no dog but a fox.

I wonder if you've ever chased any creature in your life. Seems to me you must have. The instinct must be there. Boar hunting, after all, is in your genes.

Not that I'm not glad we're all peaceable kingdom here. I wouldn't have it any other way.

Just remembered my old boyfriend training Beau to sit still for a full minute with a pet mouse on his head.

I *have* seen you snap at flies and other insects, to my worry including stinging ones. And you once ate an enormous spider before I could stop you.

Or maybe it was the mouse being trained to sit with a dog under its butt.

The other constant sound here is the surf, which I like to think is as restful for you as it is for me.

The first time we went down to the beach I wondered if you'd ever seen the ocean before, or gone swimming, or walked on sand. (The size of your footprints I imagine giving some people pause.) Luckily, the beach is just minutes away. We go only when the sun is low, early morning or dusk. Short as it is, the walk's not always easy for you. You go slowly, ever more slowly—*hobble* is the word I'm dodging here. I'm afraid that one day we'll get down there all right but then you won't be able to make it back.

In the city a short time ago a scary thing happened. It was scorching, the first really bad day of the season, and we were headed for the shade of the park. But before we could get there, and though we hadn't gone far, you stopped, you buckled and sank to the concrete, clearly distressed.

I nearly panicked, thought I was going to lose you right then right there.

How kind people were. Someone dashed into a coffee bar and came back with a bowl of cold water, which you drank greedily without getting up. Then a woman passing by stopped, took out an umbrella, and stood holding it open to shield you from the sun; it's okay if I'm late for work, she said. A man driving by offered us a ride, but I knew you'd have trouble climbing into the backseat, and by then thankfully you'd revived and we were able to walk home.

Now every time I walk you my heart is in my throat.

But you must walk, the vet says. You must get at least some exercise every day.

The medication is working, he tells me. The pain relievers and anti-inflammatories ensure that, though you may not always be totally comfortable, you are not in agony. Which could change, of course, and *that* is an agony to *me*. Because how will I know.

Haunted by Ackerley's description of Queenie at the end: *She began to turn her face to the wall, to turn her back to me.* That was the moment, the sign he took to mean he should have her— killed.

You'll let me know, won't you. Remember, I'm only human, I'm nowhere near as sharp as you are. I'll need a sign when it gets to be too much.

I don't see it as tampering with nature, playing God, or, as some would have it, interfering with a being's spiritual journey, its passage to the bardo. I see it as a blessing. I want for you what I'd want for myself.

And I'll be there, of course. I'll be with you on that last journey to the vet.

I thought the moment had come yesterday, when you left your breakfast untouched. I broke off a piece of my own breakfast bread, which you ate from my hand. (*Like reading mass together.*) By evening, though, your appetite had returned.

So let's think no more about it. Let's look to this day, and only this day. This gift of a perfect summer morning.

One more summer. At least you got that.

One more summer to lie stretched out and contented in the sun.

And at least I get to say good-bye.

Am I talking to you, or to myself? I confess the line has gotten blurred.

The weeks before we came here were so hard. It's been some time since you could make it comfortably up and down five flights of stairs, and so we'd started taking the elevator. This was mostly fine with the neighbors. By now they're used to seeing us, and only one person, a retired nurse whose husband died of leukemia last year, has questioned your designation as a therapy animal. But even she has commented on how well mannered you are, the way you scrunch your body so as not to take up too much of the elevator's tight space. And other tenants, much like people we meet all the time, are plainly delighted when they see you, charmed in the way people often are by any type of gentle giant.

But the increasingly pungent odor of your coat, the stench of your breath and ropy drool—particularly in that close space, now suffocating in the heat—were harder and harder to ignore.

And then: the dreaded inevitable. In the elevator, in the hallway, in the carpeted lobby. Hardly a day passed without an accident. And nowhere was the problem worse than in the apartment. Jesus, it smells like a stable, said a delivery man. Someone else said zoo. Hector, God bless him, said nothing.

Three rugs, the couch, and the bed had to go. I got a second rubber air mattress, and we started sleeping side by side on the two mattresses on the floor.

I did my best, vigorously mopping and scrubbing, going through several bottles of Lysol a week. But the job began to seem herculean, and the odor never really went away. It has permeated the wood floors, the bookshelves. It's in all my clothes— the way cigarette smoke was when I was in my twenties—and, I sometimes fear, in my skin and hair.

It's bad but not *that* bad, said the person who's always been most sympathetic about my situation. What you need to do is get away for a while, let the place air out.

Just when I was about to despair, he came to our rescue.

My mom had to go into a nursing home, he said. She's got this cottage on Long Island where she used to spend summers. We just sold it, but the new owners don't take possession till after Labor Day. They're planning to gut the place and completely renovate it, so it won't really matter what damage the dog does. And he can be outdoors a lot of the time anyway. I didn't get out there much myself this summer. I've got to work, and I hate being a weekender, especially in August, traffic's such a bitch. Anyway, it's only two more weeks, and you need it more than I do. Your life will be so much easier there, you'll see. While you're gone, if you want, I'll see what I can do about your apartment.

My hero.

Even chauffeured us here in his SUV.

Getting you into the SUV without hurting you was one more hurdle. Hector came up with a makeshift ramp: an old door that had been stashed in the building basement.

No stairs for us to worry about here, just two little steps to the porch. And no need for a car. I can bike the six miles to town to do grocery shopping. A week from today, when we have to leave, our friend will come in his SUV and drive us home.

The first night here there was a spectacular storm. We cowered together under a roof that sounded like it was being strafed. Rain all night, and in the morning calm. It was like some membrane had been peeled away to reveal a whole new world, bright and clean. You could almost hear Schubert's "Ave Maria." You could almost smell the blue. And every day since has been glorious.

On the beach, usually around dusk, we sometimes see another pair: a young man, shirtless, caramel tan, ice-blond hair— a real beach boy—and his Weimaraner. We watch the dog plunge into the water to fetch the stick the man keeps throwing for him. The man has an arm. Far, far out sails the stick. Far, far out swims the dog, again and again, breasting wave after wave, tireless. A thrilling sight. How deliriously happy he seems, how triumphant, racing back to drop the stick at the man's feet.

I can't suppress a throb of envy as I watch these two strong young creatures play. But that's me. *You* watch with your habitual calm. You know nothing of envy. No yearnings, or nostalgia. No regrets. You really are a different species.

I thought the time would pass more slowly, given how idle I've been. Reading Elmore Leonard, binge-watching *Game of Thrones*, doing some prep for teaching—that's about it. Living on sandwiches, mostly, and too lazy even to make them, pick up two a day from the deli, some fruit from the farm stand, enough.

Hour after hour I have sat on this porch, just thinking. For example, about the therapist—remember him? I've been thinking about some things he said. Suicide is contagious. One of the strongest predictors of suicide is knowing a suicide. Of course I knew where he was going. Doctor Obvious. I remember telling him about my dream, the man in the dark coat, in the snow. Was he beckoning—hurry up, hurry hurry—or was he warning me away?

I was thinking about this because I had that same dream again a few nights ago. Only this time, instead of an empty field of snow, it was some kind of battleground we were on. Bombs exploding, soldiers aiming and firing. And this time it was a full-blown nightmare.

It's common clinical practice to ask a person who's talking suicide to describe how they would go about it. The more specific the plan, the louder the alarm. Now, if it was me ready to say good-bye cruel world, I'd be in just the right place. Throw myself in the ocean, swim away from shore as far as I could.

Which would not be far. I am such a bad swimmer I've never been in water over my head.

But didn't I hear that drowning is the worst way to die? I'm sure I read this somewhere. Question is, how do they know?

The one experience she would never describe.

Say—Sea—Take me. Is the poet talking about Love, or Death?

Nothing has changed. It's still very simple. I miss him. I miss him every day. I miss him very much.

But how would it be if that feeling was gone?

I would not want that to happen.

I told the shrink: It would not make me happy at all not to miss him anymore.

You can't hurry love, as the song goes. You can't hurry grief, either.

I have this idea that he did what others before him have been known to do: convinced himself that those he left behind would be all right. We'd be in shock for a while, and then we'd grieve for a while, and then we'd get over it, as people do. The world doesn't end, life always moves on, and we too would move on, doing whatever we had to do.

And if that's what *he* had to do in order not to suffer, on top of everything else, the pain of guilt, that's all right with me. That's all right with me.

Sure I worried that writing about it might be a mistake. You write a thing down because you're hoping to get a hold on it. You write about experiences partly to understand what they mean, partly not to lose them to time. To oblivion. But there's always the danger of the opposite happening. Losing the memory of the experience itself to the memory of writing about it. Like people whose memories of places they've traveled to are in fact only memories of the pictures they took there. In the end, writing and photography probably destroy more of the past than they ever preserve of it. So it could happen: by writing about someone lost—or even just talking too much about them—you might be burying them for good.

The thing is, even now, I still can't say for certain whether or not I was in love with him. I've been in love no few times, and never any doubt about it. But him— Well, what does it matter now. Who can say. What is love? It's like a mystic's attempt to define faith that I remember reading somewhere: *It's not this, it's not that. It's like this, but it's not this. It's like that, but it's not that.*

But it's not true that nothing's changed. Not that I'd use words like *healing* or *recovery* or *closure*, but I am aware of something different. Something that feels like a preparation, maybe. Not there yet but on the verge of some release. A letting go.

Text message: *How are you? Your apt now shipshape!*

My hero.

Now I'm thinking about the woman whose house this is. Was. A woman I've never met. Except for the bare essentials, the three little rooms have been cleared out. Left behind, probably by mistake: a silver-framed black-and-white photograph hanging on the bedroom wall. A couple, no doubt she and her husband, standing by a car. (Why did people back then always pose for pictures standing by a car?) He in his US Army uniform, she in the style of the day: big shoulders, victory rolls, Minnie Mouse pumps. Handsome/pretty. Young. Just kids. I know that he died more than a decade ago. It seems she'd been managing very well alone until last year, when everything started failing at once. From an energetic swimmer and gardener and crack crossword-puzzle solver she's become all but helpless. No legs, no eyes, no ears, no teeth, no wind. Almost no memory. Less and less mind.

When did she plant the roses. In full magnificent bloom now, the red and the white. A fragrance to make you go, *Aaah*. I think how much they must have pleased her, year after year, and made her proud. And it's not the thought that she must miss them, but that she's no longer capable of missing them, that makes me sad. What we miss—what we lose and what we mourn—isn't it this that makes us who, deep down, we truly are. To say nothing of what we wanted in life but never got to have.

Definitely true past a certain age. And that age younger than people might like to think.

I see the sun has knocked you out. But let's not overdo it, eh. It's supposed to go up to ninety today.

Maybe I should get you some water. And while I'm at it a nice tall glass of iced tea for myself.

Oh, look at that. Butterflies. A whole swarm of them, floating like a small white cloud across the lawn. I don't think I've ever seen so many flying together like that, though it's not unusual to see them in pairs. Cabbage whites, I think. Too far to tell if there are black dots on the wings.

They should watch out for you, o eater of insects. One snap of those jaws would take out most of them. But there they go, heading right for you, as if you were no more than a giant rock lying in the grass. They shower you like confetti, and you—not a twitch!

Oh, what a sound. What could that gull have seen to make it cry out like that?

The butterflies are in the air again, moving off, in the direction of the shore.

I want to call your name, but the word dies in my throat.

Oh, my friend, my friend!

ACKNOWLEDGMENTS

Thank you, Joy Harris. Thank you, Sarah McGrath.

I am also grateful to the Civitella Ranieri Foundation, the Saltonstall Foundation for the Arts, and Hedgebrook for their generous support.

An excerpt of this book appeared in *The Paris Review*. Thank you, Lorin Stein.